The Price to Love
Paperback Copyright © 2022 Lorhainne Ekelund

Editor: Talia Leduc

ISBN-13: 978-1998775460

Give feedback on the book at:
lorhainneeckhart@hotmail.com

Twitter: @LEckhart
Facebook: AuthorLorhainneEckhart

Printed in the U.S.A

The Price to Love

THE FRIESSEN LEGACY

THE FRIESSENS: A NEW BEGINNING
BOOK TWO

LORHAINNE ECKHART

The Friessen Family Series
Reading order:

The Outsider Series

The Forgotten Child
A Baby And A Wedding
Fallen Hero
The Awakening
Secrets
Runaway
Overdue
The Unexpected Storm
The Wedding

The Friessens: A New Beginning

The Deadline
The Price to Love
A Different Kind of Love
A Vow of Love, A Friessen Family Christmas

The Friessens

The Friessen Family

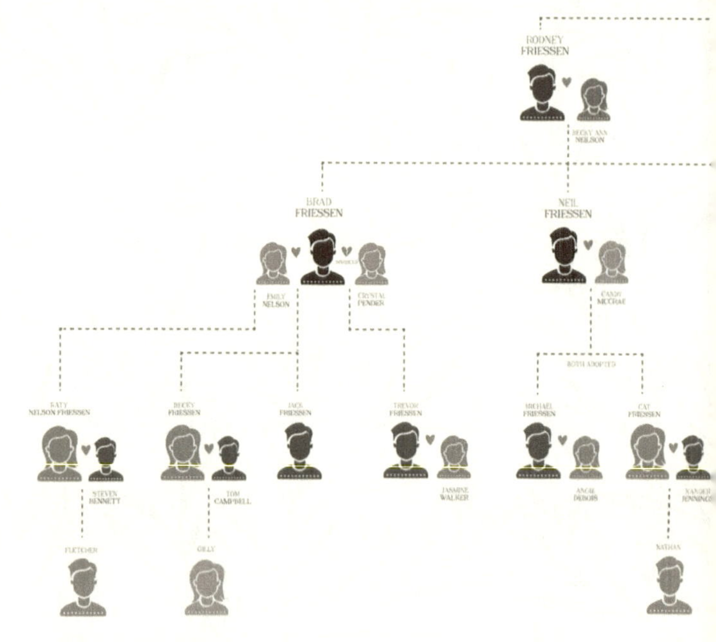

The Outsider Series

THE FORGOTTEN CHILD	BRAD & EMILY
A BABY AND A WEDDING	BRAD & EMILY & and Jed and the Rodney & Becky
FALLEN HERO	JED, DIANA & ANDY
THE SEARCH	JED, DIANA & ANDY
THE AWAKENING	ANDY & LAURA

The Outsider Series

SECRETS	DIANA & JED with the entire Friessen Family
RUNAWAY	ANDY & LAURA
OVERDUE	JED & DIANA
THE UNEXPECTED STORM	NEIL & CANDY
THE WEDDING	NEIL & CANDY and the entire Friessen Family

The Friessens: A New Beginning

THE DEADLINE	ANDY & LAURA
THE PRICE TO LOVE	NEIL & CANDY
A DIFFERENT KIND OF LOVE	BRAD & EMILY
A VOW OF LOVE	THE ENTIRE
A FRIESSEN FAMILY CHRISTMAS	FRIESSEN FAMILY

The Friessens

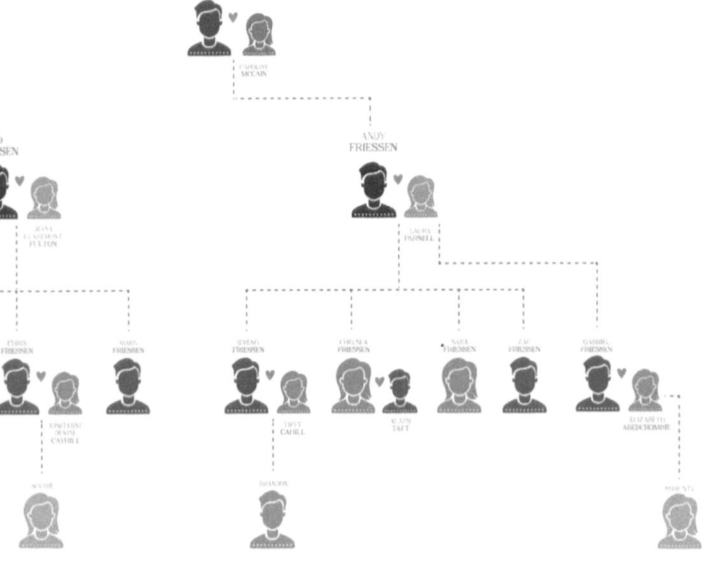

TODD FRIESSEN
CAROLINE McCAIN
ANDY FRIESSEN
LAURA DARNELL
JED FRIESSEN
DIANA CLAREMONT FULTON
CHRIS FRIESSEN
JOSEPHINE DENISE CAYHILL
MARY FRIESSEN
JEREMY FRIESSEN
TIFFY CAHILL
CHELSEA FRIESSEN
ALARIC TAFT
SARA FRIESSEN
ZAC FRIESSEN
GABRIEL FRIESSEN
ELIZABETH ABERCROMBIE
SOPHIE
BRANDON
SHAUNTY

The Price to Love

'A 2015 READERS' FAVORITE AWARD WINNER'

—*"The Price to Love is an emotional story about a marriage on the brink of falling apart and how two people cope with changing relationships."*

5 STAR REVIEW FROM NATASHA JACKSON READERS' FAVORITE

— *"Lorhainne Eckhart, is courageous to write a story with a "good guy" who is so despicable in his behavior. That does not ruin the story, though; if anything, it adds realism and volume to the plot."*

SUSAN

—*"Any book that has me wanting to cry and yell at the characters this much ... a story that holds me to it so much I don't want to put it down ... .THAT is a good book!"*

LORNA

—"I don't know if I should love him or hate him, but I couldn't put it down"

A. CUSTOMER

—"I loved this emotional roller coaster."

MIMI BARBOUR, NEW YORK TIMES BESTSELLING AUTHOR

—"I was pulled in on the first page and could not put it down until I got to the last page. I love when a writer tells the story about a complete family."—Susan, Reviewer

SUSAN, REVIEWER

She could give him everything except the one thing he wanted—A child.

Candy knows that her husband wants a baby, but she can't give him one. When Neil pays for a surrogate and moves her into their home, he tells her not to worry, but she suddenly feels as if she's on the outside looking in.

Then, one day, she meets a little girl who steals her heart, a little girl with a damaged, scarred soul filled with the kind of despair and hopelessness that should never be in the innocent eyes of a child. But neither Neil nor his family understand her need to help.

As their marriage hangs on brink of disaster Candy is forced to make a choice between her husband and helping this child.

Chapter 1

There was something about the breeze, the way it drifted across the bay in harmony with the waves as they slapped against the sandy shore. It was stirring, peaceful, and powerful being this close to the salty spray of the ocean, and it helped clear her head. Candy Friessen rolled her shoulders and breathed in the fresh morning air as she walked beside Sable, her smoky gray Azteca and best friend ... though she could never tell her husband that she considered her horse her closest confidant!

Neil Friessen would never understand, because the fact was that he believed her world should rotate around him, not in an arrogant, conceited way but more a way that showed her devotion to him and their family. Neil was so committed to family—his family, his picture-perfect idea of how his family should look. Candy knew he believed they were as close as two human beings could be, and he thought of her as his best friend. He was her husband, her lover, and, at times, her confidant, but there were still some painful parts of herself that she couldn't share with him.

Those fears and dark thoughts she could only share with Sable.

Neil wanted to be a father more than anything. It was his dream, his burning desire, to have a family—but it was the one thing Candy couldn't give him; a child, *his* child. That had been taken from her at her darkest hour, when she had been left barren after an emergency hysterectomy was performed to save her life. She had been so young! She knew it wasn't fair, but she'd learned to live with this agonizing, hollow feeling deep inside; though it was an emptiness she couldn't share with her husband, only Sable, who understood the deepest parts of her soul, the things she couldn't say to anyone.

She also knew there were still options if they wanted to have a family. One door had closed while another had opened. The doctors, and their family, all meaning well, had said so—but Candy knew her husband well enough to realize that his dream of having a child of his own was the one thing that would always come between them. Oh, he loved her. She knew that, as he wouldn't have married her once she'd given him the opportunity to walk away. She wondered, though, if there were times he regretted what he'd done. Maybe she was reading too much into it, but this was what she did on her mornings alone with Sable as they walked side by side down their sandy white Cancun beach.

When she tossed around the idea of what was next in their journey, it always came down to one thing—how much she loved Neil. To stop loving him would be like suffocating herself. She couldn't do it. She loved her magnetic, charming, and powerful husband—and he was *hers*. Every time he was with her, he touched her, talked to her, took over her thoughts and senses. His hold over her was unsettling, now that she was away from him and had the space to think, but she had to admit there was some-thing addictive about him giving her all his attention. He knew how to look after himself, too, which added to the attraction and the dynamics between them. Of course, his confidence and inner strength made her believe he would always take care of everything. He made her feel safe, loved, and cared for … as if she were in a bubble that could burst at any moment.

Neil Friessen was everything to her, and the man still had the ability to take her breath away. She just wished she could be as confident in their love, especially considering Neil was oblivious to the fact that any warm and breathing woman would have given him a second look, doing every-thing she could to get closer to him. It bothered Candy, though she knew this was a sign of a lack of faith on her part. Neil was smart and loving, always holding her hand and waking her with a wild, burning passion every morn-ing, and she loved all of that about him, but she still couldn't tell him about this feeling she had, this building confusion, as if something was about to change everything —all because of what he was proposing now—a surrogate. He had mentioned it the night before, out of the blue, but just the idea of another woman carrying his child was too much to bear. Candy shut her eyes at the thought of another woman stepping in to do something she couldn't. It left her feeling impossibly lonely.

Sable nudged her shoulder as they walked side by side down their beach until the resort, in full construction, came into view. She stumbled and slowed at the chaos of the pounding, the constant buzz of power tools, creaky scaffolding, and workers. She stopped by the fence that was the gateway to her private beach—and to Neil's multimil-lion-dollar resort. He was erecting it where her house had once been, the property owned by her father, which he had left to her when he died. What had once been there had been swept away by a storm the previous year.

It had been her land, though she had lost it to her creditors. Neil had coveted that land for years, but after buying and paying for it, he'd given it back to her. It had been a gift of love, and she hadn't been able to deny her husband his dream. The beachfront resort he was now building had once been an obstacle between them, but she trusted him to do what was best for the land because of how much she loved him.

Candy looped the lead rope around Sable's neck and slid the halter around his muzzle and over his nose before tying it at the post. He was starting to skitter from the noise, and their connection had been lost. She held him steady when a sudden bang had her heart racing and Sable spooking. "It's all right, Sable," she murmured. "Let's turn around and head back home and away from this noise."

It was loud and chaotic, a huge project that provided jobs to a community that desperately needed them. She understood that, but it was hard to let go of what had once been. The tide had turned, changing her life in ways she could never have imagined. She had once fought this sort of change, but her love for Neil had helped her overcome her fears.

"Candy!" she heard her husband call out, and she picked up their pace, starting back down the beach until she spotted him.

He was dressed so neat and tidy, with dress pants and a white shirt. His dark hair was neatly groomed, and he walked purposefully toward her. "I've been looking everywhere for you," he said. "Why didn't you tell me you were taking your horse out and coming down here to the beach?"

She kept walking toward him. It was always his eyes,

their intensity, that reached out to her and pulled her to him. She could never look away—even though being with Neil, being his wife, sometimes made her feel as if she were drowning.

"Next time, let me know if you're coming down here," he said. He glanced over her shoulder at the fence and the workers on the other side; there was something in his expression that had her looking back.

"Neil, I always came down here before," she said. What was going on? At times, Neil could be overbearing and overprotective; it stoked her temper, but there was something about the way he watched the workers that bothered her.

"I don't want you down here alone anymore. Can't that just be the end of it, Candy? Why do you have to question everything?" Neil said, sounding annoyed.

This was so unlike him, and she found herself watching him the way she would Sable, trying to figure out what was going on. He sighed and shook his head, gesturing toward the construction.

"I didn't mean to say it like that," he said. "I just can't explain it. There're a lot of riffraff around right now, workers coming in from all around Mexico, and I haven't had the chance to get to know any of them yet. I don't want to be worrying about you right now, and I don't want something to happen to you. Do you understand?" He stepped closer to her, and Sable nudged him as he put his hands on her shoulders. His eyes slid down, and she knew he was taking in her very short white shorts, white tank top, and sneakers. He lifted her long, dark hair over her shoulders and tucked strands behind her ear. For a moment in time, it was just them. "Tell me you'll listen to me," he said, "just this once."

How could she deny him when he looked at her the

way he did, as if she was the only thing that existed for him in that moment?

"You know how much I love this; the beach, the ocean, spending time with Sable," she said. "I need to do this every morning. It's who I am, Neil, and you agreed to keep this part of the beach ours."

He touched her cheek and rubbed the pad of his thumb over her lips as he tilted his head closer, really taking her in. It was distracting, he had to know. "I promise I'll come down with you every day," he said. "It's just not safe right now. It won't always be like this, Candy. I promise."

She could smell his minty breath. She could feel his warmth even though his lips hadn't touched hers yet.

He took a deep breath and said, "I got a call from a possible surrogate."

She couldn't help the way her body instantly stiffened.

Thankfully, Neil didn't appear to have noticed, as his hand slipped away and dropped to his side. He stepped back, looking impossibly happy. "She'd like to meet us in an hour."

She felt as if she were being sucked into a vortex. Her ears rang as she watched joy fill his expression. She hadn't even had time to digest the idea, and now he was barreling right ahead as if he wanted no further discussion. No matter how hard she tried, she couldn't see eye to eye with him on this. Why did he always have to move so quickly on his ideas?

Maybe her feelings were showing, as his smile faded and his expression became serious. "What's wrong?" he asked.

"I just don't understand why you feel a surrogate is the only answer. I mean, you haven't even considered adoption, and there's an orphanage so close by. There're a lot of children, young children, who need parents, Neil."

"Candy, you know how I feel," he said. "I want a baby, a child of my own. You already know that with an international adoption, there would be a waitlist, interviews, red tape. We're Americans, Candy. As difficult as it would be to adopt in the U.S, we wouldn't even know what we were getting into here. We'd be old by the time a baby became available. No, this is better; less mess, fewer problems."

She wanted to finish for him, to say what she knew he was really thinking. He wanted a child with his blood, his genes, one that was biologically his. If there was one thing about Neil Friessen, it was that when he wanted something, he never allowed anything to stand in his way.

"I see. So your mind is made up?" She swallowed the lump that had formed in her throat.

"Candy, we've discussed this. We've already decided. I know you want a baby. I saw how much you loved looking after the babies when we stayed in Montana at Andy and Laura's. You have no idea how happy I was to see how comfortable you were with Chelsea. You loved holding her. I could see how much you wanted a baby. Let me give that to you."

"Neil, I loved caring for Chelsea and Jeremy. Your cousin's twins are adorable babies. But I'm also a realist. I think we need to talk about other ways. You only mentioned surrogacy last night! I need time to digest this, to discuss all the aspects of it with you. I need to be comfortable with this entire process."

She could feel him pull back even though he hadn't moved one step. He looked away and sighed. She knew he felt disappointed, annoyed, frustrated—the same way he felt whenever he couldn't get her to think his way. She was smart enough to let him believe he'd convinced her, and she remembered what his mother had once said: *The Friessen men are so strong, both physically and emotionally, that , at times, it would have been easy to lose herself.*

"Candy, why do you have to argue and overanalyze everything when a good thing comes along?" he said. "Sometimes you just have to go with it. Please don't fight this, baby. Let's talk to her. We'll figure it out."

He went to reach for the lead rope to take Sable from her, but she held tight and started walking. "So where are we meeting this woman?" she asked, swallowing again. This feeling, whatever it was, had stirred up all her vulnerabilities; the ones she thought she'd put to rest long ago.

"Here," he said. "She's coming to the house."

Every nerve in Candy's body zinged, and she stopped suddenly. Sable picked up on her shock, prancing and raising his head. Neil reached for the rope before Candy could gather herself and took it from her hand.

"Let's go," he said. "You have enough time to get cleaned up and put on something nice." He started walking away with her horse. "Candy, come on," he called out over his shoulder.

Candy watched as Neil walked away. He was her husband, who had taken over everything and in turn had provided her with a life any woman would give her right arm for. For some reason that she couldn't explain, their marriage was snowballing into something else, and she realized she was quickly losing who she was—losing her sense of self and her ability to stand on her own two feet. It bothered her because he was making it so easy for her to slip into that role of being cared for, allowing him to handle everything. The problem was, that if something ever happened to Neil and she found herself alone, she would be more vulnerable than ever.

Chapter 2

Candy stared at the simple but tasteful white dress with cap sleeves that Neil had put on the bed for her. A pair of strappy gold sandals sat on the floor. He loved dressing her, picking out her clothes when they went out. Neil Friessen was a sharply dressed man, who loved a sharply dressed woman, and Candy would be the first to admit that her husband had much better taste in clothes than she did.

She sat on the stool in front of the mirror in their large master bedroom, glancing into the en suite bathroom, brightly lit by the sun flowing through the skylights and windows. Then there was the walk-in closet, with shelves and racks full of clothes, many she'd never even worn. She still couldn't get used to Neil believing she needed so many outfits. Before Neil, her wardrobe had consisted of a few jeans, t-shirts, a summer skirt—barely enough to fill three small drawers in a dresser, really. But this was just one aspect of her eccentric, complicated husband.

Today, as she sat perched on the stool, she just couldn't bring herself to pick up the dress laid over the gold comforter of their four-poster bed. It was too fancy for just meeting a woman who might possibly carry her husband's child. She was still stunned over what Neil had brought up the night before. As she was getting ready for bed, he had mentioned the surrogacy as if it were just another aspect of their search. A young woman would be implanted with a donated egg, and fertilized by his semen, all done in a lab. It would be clinical, with no emotion involved. Then the woman would give birth and simply walk away. A contract would be signed, she would be paid, and they would have their baby. The entire time Neil spoke, saying over and over that this was the right way to go, rambling off the legal aspects (which, of course, her mind had tuned out), she had said nothing—until he asked what she thought about his idea.

As she took in the happiness and joy beaming from him, she had been reminded of the time she took a home pregnancy test … before her ectopic pregnancy changed everything for them. This wouldn't be her carrying his baby, a love child. It would be another woman. All Candy had been able to say was that surrogacy was, of course, another aspect they could consider. She'd never meant for this to be the only option. She'd thought they would have time to talk about other avenues. What was his rush? From that one comment, had he decided she was in favor of this ridiculous idea and wanted him to go ahead and find a surrogate?

She tried to remember everything they had discussed, because she was positive a step had been missed—namely, he had neglected to consult her about this very important decision. She glanced at the clock and sighed at the time she had wasted. Instead of changing, she ran a brush through her hair and rummaged through her closet, grabbing the first blouse she touched. It was a new one Neil had bought her a week ago, with blue and orange flowers on sheer white fabric; she pulled it on over her white tank top so that it hung loosely past her hips. She glanced at her makeup, which was organized neatly in the drawers, and stepped away. She never wore makeup, not unless she needed to attend one of Neil's important business functions. The first time, he had hired someone to show her how to apply it.

She glanced in the mirror at her lightly tanned complexion, and the hint of natural pink in her cheeks. She looked fine—more than fine. She didn't believe she needed to coat her face with all that color, so she slipped her bare feet into flat sandals, the comfortable ones she wore every day, and started down the ceramic tile stairs, taking in the grand entry, the faded orange adobe walls. Her husband was talking to someone, and she noticed Ana carrying a tray with a pitcher and glasses into the living room.

Neil had his back to Candy as she strode quietly across the foyer. He was folding up a newspaper and tucking it in a box by the fireplace. He looked so professional in his crisp white dress shirt, navy dress pants, and leather belt. The way he dressed screamed class and wealth, but at least he hadn't put on a tie. Candy went down the two wide ceramic steps into their large, warm living room, decorated in browns and greens, with large windows overlooking the grounds. It was the room in the house where the family, including Neil's parents, Rodney and Becky, gathered most nights before dinner.

Neil, Rodney and Becky owned this ten-thousand-acre estate, which had some of the best cattle ranching around these parts. It was a business venture Neil and Rodney shared, and there was a ranch house and camp at the far west side of the property, which held, at last count, five hundred head of cattle. A foreman and cook lived there all year, and the cowboys they hired stayed in the camp and never came to this side of the property. Neil had only taken her there once. She knew he didn't like the interest the ranch hands had shown, although they were just being friendly. Neil didn't like other men showing interest in what he believed was his, so that one time had been the first and last.

"Mister Neil, when are you expecting your guest?" Ana asked. The short, plump Mayan woman was their house-keeper and cook, and she moved a plate of cookies onto the sofa table.

"Any minute now," Neil replied as he glanced at his watch before noticing Candy where she lingered beside the bookshelf. "Candy, I didn't hear you come in," he said. His gaze lingered on her as he took in what she was wearing. His expression was questioning. This was the first time she had chosen something different than what he'd set out for her. Before, it had been helpful for him to pick out her clothes when she didn't know what to wear, but now it seemed as if he was dressing her up to meet a mistress. She said nothing.

"Your parents, will they be meeting this woman, as well?" Ana asked.

Neil turned to Ana, distracted, and said, "No, not yet." He stepped around the sofa, closer to Candy, and Ana took that moment to slip out of the room. "Why aren't you wearing the dress that I set out for you?" he asked.

"I didn't want to wear a dress. What's wrong with what I'm wearing?"

"You're not wearing makeup, so what have you been doing for the past hour?" He sounded annoyed.

"I was thinking," she said as she moved around the sofa

toward one of the large windows. She leaned in and stared at the small black car pulling up out front.

"What were you thinking about?" he asked. She could feel his heat as he stepped up behind her.

She shrugged. "Just some things. Besides, what should it matter what I wear? Is there something more going on, here?"

This time she met his gaze, and humor filled his expression. She wasn't amused, though. She was ready for a fight, though their fights usually led her to a place she loved to be—making up with him in bed. He put his hands on his hips, and she knew he was about to start in on her and maybe push a little harder. He never let things go, not after everything they'd been through, fighting their way back to each other from hell. Her connection with Neil was everything she'd every wanted, but at times his worry about her could be smothering.

Fortunately, he was stopped from pushing his agenda, as far as dressing her went, when the doorbell rang. Candy glanced out the window and noticed two women as Neil yelled out, "I'll get it, Ana."

She didn't move from her spot by the window as he went down the hall. Charm oozed from her husband as he spoke, and then, as expected, she heard a woman laughing. Neil had that effect. She rolled her eyes, knowing no one could see her, and listened to their voices and footsteps as they approached.

"Candy, this is Maria and her mother, Carmen," Neil said as they entered. The two women stood beside Neil and followed him after he gestured to the sofas. "Come in, sit down, please. Could I offer you a glass of lemonade?"

"Si, senor. That is very kind," the older woman said. She was slim and attractive, with jet-black hair woven with silver threads, pinned back at the sides with two barrettes.

She was pretty and looked so neat and tidy in her red skirt and white blouse. Her daughter, Maria, was a young woman, and she smiled brightly up at Neil. When her gaze slid over to Candy, she blushed. Her hair was long, dark, straight—not wild and out of control, like Candy's. She was slim, with long legs, and curvy in a way men must have loved.

Neil poured two glasses of lemonade, and Maria smiled in a coy, shy way that stirred all Candy's insecurities. Her stomach was starting to hurt, maybe from how tightly she'd been holding on to everything, bottling up her feelings. Having a woman here who would carry her husband's child … it was almost more than she could bear.

"Candy?" Neil gestured to another glass as he poured.

"No," she said, shaking her head and crossing her arms in front of her. She took only one step from her spot by the window before deciding to stay where she was.

Neil set the glass down and strode around to the fireplace, facing the women. "I'm glad you agreed to come. My wife isn't able to have children, and we want a family —a child of our own."

Maria, sitting right beside her mother, cast Candy a sympathetic look, and Carmen patted her daughter's hand. "My Maria is strong and young. She can carry your child, Mister Friessen," she said boldly.

Candy had never considered that Neil would talk openly about her condition this way, in front of strangers, and it stung—never mind the fact that this was why the women were here in the first place. "How old are you, Maria?" she asked.

Everyone turned her way. Maybe they'd forgotten she was there. She couldn't help feeling like a third wheel, considering how Carmen darted a glance between her and

Neil as if she'd already figured out who made the decisions in their relationship.

"Maria is nineteen," Carmen said with authority, as if talking down to Candy.

Candy started around the easy chair closest to Neil. "That's very young for what you're offering to do. I wonder if you've really considered all the ramifications," she said. She didn't need to look at Neil to know he wasn't pleased, but at least he wasn't saying anything to undermine her—well, not yet, anyway. "Maria," she continued, "have you thought about what might happen if you become pregnant and decide you can't go through with it? I mean, you'll carry a baby inside you for nine months and then be expected to walk away and have no contact with the child. Are you telling me, honestly, that you can do that?"

Maria's smile faded. She was watching Candy with an odd look in her light brown eyes. There was something there that was young and old at the same time. She was beautiful, and her face had a radiance that Candy found attractive. There was innocence, but also something that suggested this young woman was experienced beyond her age. Then again, perhaps Candy might have been reading too much into her expression. It was an awkward situation.

"Of course it won't be easy, but, to me, this is a gift, something I can offer a childless couple who could give their child everything," she said.

"You'll be paid, though, of course," Candy added.

Carmen turned, giving Candy all her attention. "My Maria understands, very clearly, what this is about." She gestured with the flat of her hand to Neil. "My daughter will sign your contract, and you will pay for all medical care and living expenses, and she will be compensated for her time. This is a business arrangement, nothing more," she said.

The woman was blunt, and Candy watched Maria closely as her mother spoke for her. The young lady glanced at her hands, which were folded together in her lap, her expression neutral, giving nothing away. Candy wondered what was really going on in her head.

"We won't begin anything until the contract is signed and all the terms are agreed to," Neil said. "My lawyer will handle all the details, and there's mandatory counseling, as well."

Candy wondered if her shock showed on her face. Why was this the first time she was hearing of this? She wanted to pull Neil aside and say something, but she realized, as she looked back at Carmen, who was watching her intently, that the sharp woman had picked up on her confusion.

"Yes, we understand the counseling, but perhaps your wife does not?" she said.

To Candy, her words sounded callous and undermining, but Neil must have interpreted her another way, as he looked to Candy, stepping closer and sliding his arm around her waist. "My wife understands everything," he said. He held her tightly for a moment, and she wondered whether he had picked up on how stiff she was as she did everything to hold herself together and not snap at him. He walked over to the sofa table and picked up some papers she hadn't even noticed were sitting there. "This is the contract—what is expected of you and what you can expect from me. Take the time to carefully look it over so that you understand what you'd be agreeing to. This will be overseen by my attorney, of course, but you're welcome to have your own lawyer look over the contract. I think you'll see that I've been extremely generous."

Neil held out the contract to Maria. She hesitated for a moment, maybe wondering whether she should take it. When her mother went to reach for it, Neil pulled back. "No, I'm sorry, Carmen. This contact must be agreed to in its entirety by your daughter. She needs to understand clearly her responsibilities, otherwise this won't work. You're welcome to support your daughter and be there for her emotionally, but the details of this must be understood and agreed to solely by her."

Carmen pulled back in her seat and gestured to Maria. "I wouldn't have it any other way. Maria, take the papers. You need to read them over."

Candy just watched the exchange. Her alarm bells were going off. There was something about the mother and daughter that seemed problematic. Neil was so astute in business, but when she looked over at him, his expression was that of a man pleased with where things were headed. What was wrong with him? He would have been all over this if it had been some ordinary business deal.

"Thank you for coming by. If I could have your answer by Friday?" Neil added.

This time, Maria stood up and said, "Of course, Mister Friessen—"

"Neil," he said, interrupting her with his characteristic warmth. "Please call me Neil."

"Neil, yes. I will read this carefully, but if you would like my answer now, it's yes. I can't imagine it changing. I just knew when I spoke with you on the phone that you sounded like a nice man, and now, meeting your wife … well, I'm very excited."

She had talked to him on the phone? Candy couldn't hide the warmth in her cheeks, so she turned away, not considering how rude it would appear. She needed to have more than a few words with Neil. This was something they needed to discuss together, not with strangers.

"Thank you, Neil—and thank you, Missus Friessen," Maria called out to her softly.

Candy turned around with her hand to her chin. The two women were watching her from the stairs, and she had to look away. She could feel Neil's eyes on her, but she wasn't about to look his way, because then he'd know how angry and hurt she was. Right now, in front of these women, that was a vulnerability she couldn't show.

Chapter 3

She couldn't believe how Neil had lingered outside with those two women, chatting as if they were good friends. Maria had giggled like a silly school-girl to everything he said, and Candy had just rolled her eyes again as she waited for her husband. When she peeked out the window and watched Maria climb into the passenger side door, with Neil helping her in before closing the door for her, her temper flared, and she had to fight back the sting of tears, blinking madly.

It was horrible, standing there, waiting for her husband to come back in and give her the time of day. A wave of guilt rushed through her. She usually wasn't needy, but she felt as if all of this baby stuff was turning her into a crazy person. She started for the stairs when she heard the car engine roar outside.

"Well, that went really well," Neil said as he walked back in and closed the door. "I have a great feeling about …"

She kept walking, not missing how his voice had trailed off.

"Where are you going?" he asked.

"Upstairs," she said, her throat aching. He was following her now, of course, letting out one of those sighs he gave when she tested his patience. This time, she wasn't interested in smoothing things over. She wanted to be alone to think. She went into their bedroom and heard their bedroom door close behind her.

"Candy, stop," he said. "Can you just tell me what's going on with you?"

She couldn't believe it, the way he was making it sound as if this problem was just about her. "Are you kidding me?" she snapped. "How do you think I felt to hear that you've already had a conversation about surrogacy with this woman over the phone? I can't believe you actually went ahead and had a contract done up. I thought this was just a meeting, or did I miss something?" She lingered on the other side of the bed, holding the foot rail, and Neil put a hand on his hip and took a stance as if he was getting ready to lay down the law. Was he actually irritated with her?

"Look, I filled you in last night," he said. "This is a great idea—even you thought so. Why wouldn't I go ahead and have an agreement drafted? If she's not going to go along with the terms, we'll look for someone else. Nothing is settled right now."

"Neil, I'm your wife, your lover, your friend—but this thing, bringing in a surrogate … this is a huge, life-altering decision. There could be huge problems you haven't even considered. You can't make a decision about this without talking to me! This is something where we need to discuss every aspect together—as husband and wife. We think together on this one, or we don't do it."

He started toward her. "Candy, you're overreacting. We

talked about this last night. How is me having a contract done up, protecting every legal aspect, wrong?"

"You'd already talked to her on the phone about the details! You led me to believe you had just scheduled an appointment, but you shouldn't have done even that without talking to me. Do you have any idea how I felt, standing there in the living room, listening to her talk about your conversation, which I knew nothing about? Had it somehow slipped your mind to even mention it this morning?"

He started to speak, but maybe he knew his expression had given him away.

"Wait," she said. "When exactly did you first talk to her?"

"Last night," he finally replied, looking as if he had been caught with his hand in the cookie jar. "Look, I'm sorry. I admit I jumped the gun, but my lawyer called, and he knew we were looking at all the options for adoption. He tossed this idea out and gave me Maria's name. I thought that, before I even mentioned it to you, I would just talk to the lady, because if it wasn't going anywhere, there was no sense in mentioning it to you." He stopped again right in front of her, not close enough to touch her. She would have moved away if he tried.

"Mentioning it to me … are you kidding me? What am I, a passing thought? I thought I was part of this marriage, Neil, not an afterthought. Were you going to pick and choose which details to share with me, with something this important?"

He was watching her now, and his expression was hard, as if he was thinking about how to respond. "Candy, I'm sorry. Maybe you're right and I did get a little ahead of myself, but this is a wonderful opportunity for us to have our family. I just wanted to cover all the bases and make this easier on you." He moved closer again, putting his hand on her arm and then his other on her hip, pulling her closer to him. "I'm sorry if I made you feel left out. That wasn't my intention," he said. When he touched her, she had a hard time staying mad at him. His hands were cupping her cheeks, his thumbs caressing her chin. "You're not a passing thought. I'm sorry."

"Neil, don't do this again. You made me feel as if I was on the outside, looking in. Do you have any idea how it makes me feel that you're considering using another woman, a surrogate, to carry your child?"

"Our child," he said. She didn't miss the passion and fire in his eyes, as if he truly believed he could make her feel as he did.

"Neil, this child will be part of you, not me. I don't even have my ovaries left. This baby will be another woman's."

"Hey, stop right there," he said. "This baby will be ours. Whatever we decide, this is our chance for a family, Candy. Let me make this happen for us. Please trust me to handle all the details. With the legalese, my lawyer will make sure we have no problems."

She wanted to believe him, she really did, but there was something about this situation that unsettled her completely.

Chapter 4

"Candy, I have to tell you, the time you've offered of yourself at this orphanage is a gift," Pastor Rafael Mendoza said. He was around Neil's age, and he had dark hair and dark eyes. He was attractive and kind, and he gave a voice to so many children who had none.

Casa Perdido, the Cancun orphanage where Candy volunteered, was home to 112 children, most of whom were unregistered, born to women who had given birth on patios or had simply been unwilling to register their children. For the past sixteen days, Candy had found herself driving into Cancun to this very orphanage, the one she had stopped in after returning from Montana, where she and Neil had looked after Andy and Laura's babies. It was there that she had fallen in love with Chelsea, who was six weeks old, and had realized she wasn't a complete failure as a future parent. Of course, Chelsea's twin brother, Jeremy, was cute, too—in a demanding, Friessen-man sort of way. But holding Chelsea for hours on end … it had filled a hole in her that she hadn't even known was empty.

After stopping in the first time and seeing the need at this local orphanage, Candy had found herself looking into the lost little faces. She didn't know how someone could come in and choose just one, so she kept coming back every day for a few hours and helping out, bringing food, bedding, anywhere she saw that there was a need. Neil had never asked where she was, not that he was around during the day, and, for some reason, she didn't feel she could share this with Rodney and Becky, either. She could be wrong, but she didn't think they'd understand how she felt.

"I wish I could do more," she said as she walked beside the pastor, who was always dressed in the same worn jeans and old t-shirt, into a large room where all the beds were situated side by side. The children slept two or three to a bed, the mattresses were old, and there were blankets on the floor for more children, with cribs in another room for toddlers. "I've ordered and paid for new beds, and I hope they'll be here by the end of the week. What else can I give you?"

She hadn't thought of the expense when she charged it to Neil's credit card. She never spent anything, but she realized she needed to say something. *Tonight,* she thought. She had to tell him that night. She couldn't put it off any longer.

"You show up every day and help in the kitchen. You're an angel, and with what you've given here, the beds … I would not want to anger your husband," Rafael said. "You should bring him down here so he can see how much you do to help these children. He'd be proud of you."

"I don't know if my husband has time, but we'll see," she said, realizing she sounded vague. This was unlike her. She wasn't so sure how happy Neil would be. She forced a smile, hoping the pastor wouldn't pursue it.

The noise level increased as they entered a large room.

A plump, aging Mexican woman sat at the front, facing older children on benches. She appeared to be teaching them how to read.

"These are the ones who can't go to school," Rafael explained. "Rosa used to be a schoolteacher, but she donates her time here now."

"Why can't these children go to school?" Candy asked.

"They're unregistered," he said. "The government will not allow it. Most of these children were born to young mothers, alcoholics and prostitutes, abandoned. No one cared enough to register them. We have no birthdate for those children, so we have to guess their ages, and—"

An awful screech came from another room. It sounded like a frantic animal.

Candy followed the pastor, who hurried into a room with half a dozen young children. One small child was the source of the noise. Her hands were flailing, and she hit an older woman in the nose as she tried to hold her still.

"She's a devil child!" The woman shouted, blood dripping from her nose.

The child rolled to the floor and scurried to a corner in her old, sack-like dress. She pulled her knees up, holding tight, and rocked back and forth, humming.

The woman started toward her, brush in hand, but Candy stepped in front of the child before she could get any closer. "No! You will not hit her," she said.

The woman looked at her as if she was crazy. "That child is a problem, Pastor," she snapped. "She belongs in an institution. She's retarded! We can't look after her, and she is scaring the other children. She doesn't listen. The other children are clean, but I can't even bathe her. I just tried to undress her, and this is what happened. She needs discipline."

Candy glanced behind her at the little girl, who

appeared to be no older than four or five. Her hair was tangled, dirty. She was small, very thin, and she glanced over at the small metal tub of water.

The pastor held out his hand for the brush. "I'm sure you did the best you can," he said, "but if she doesn't understand, how will getting angry at her help? Hitting her is never the answer, Rosita."

The woman blushed. Even though the pastor had never raised his voice, there was something about the way he spoke that made Candy sure that she'd be ashamed if she had behaved that way.

"Take a break," Rafael told the woman. He patted her arm, holding the brush in his other hand. The woman said nothing as she left the room, and Candy stood over the little girl, watching her.

"What's wrong with her?" she asked.

"We don't really know, Candy. She was found a week ago eating out of a garbage can in a very bad part of town. The man who brought her here showed her a kindness. She couldn't talk, wouldn't respond. Whatever is wrong with her, the authorities would have said it's some mental illness and locked her away."

Candy knelt down in front of the small child, who seemed to tense before she could touch her. "It's okay, honey. I'm not going to hurt you," Candy said in Spanish. She didn't try to touch her—not that she knew anything about children. She knew nothing at all. She found herself observing the girl the way she would a spooked, unpredictable horse. The child was untouchable, and the only thing Candy could use to relate to her were her techniques for working with animals.

"She's unresponsive, Candy. I don't know if we can help her. She doesn't understand. She eats like an animal, with her hands, shoving food in her mouth. If you try to stop her, give her a spoon, she throws it and goes right back to using her hands. We're over capacity now and only have beds for sixty."

"What's her name?" Candy asked, watching the little girl, who paid them no mind and continued to huddle, her face buried against her knees.

"We don't know her name. She says nothing and is quiet until … well, you saw how she reacted with Rosita. She was trying to bathe her. One of the other house mothers calls her *el gato*, since she caught a mouse."

Candy glanced up at the pastor, who wore a grim expression. "She didn't …"

"No, she didn't eat it, but would she have? I don't know," he said. "I'd never seen anything like it."

Candy slid the strap of her cloth purse down and unzipped it. "You can't call her an animal. It's not right. Cat sounds nice, though," she said. "Pastor, you can't send her away."

The girl reached out her tiny hand to touch the glittering diamond on Candy's finger. Her wedding ring was huge, and the square-cut stone had the child mesmerized as she stared at it. Candy held out her hand slowly so her ring was right in the child's line of sight, closer to her. Her tiny fingers rubbed the shiny rock again.

"Do you like how sparkly that is?" she asked.

The girl didn't respond. She didn't look up—she was engrossed with the rock Neil had put on her finger when he married her. If she sold it, she knew it would provide this orphanage enough money to feed, clothe, and see to all these children's care for a few years. It could pay for staff, for an additional building, for more beds … She found herself reaching to pull it off her finger when a hand touched her shoulder.

"Don't," Mendoza said. "Your husband's ring ... you mustn't."

She glanced up at the pastor and back down at the little girl. "But it could help so many."

"There are some lines you shouldn't cross, Candy. Your husband wouldn't be happy. This is not the answer."

"Cat ..." she whispered, wanting to reach out and touch her.

The pastor knelt down beside Candy. "Cat," he said sternly, holding a cracker packet out toward her. When the child didn't respond, he ripped open the package, and her eyes went to the crackers as he stood up, pulling them out and handing them to her. Her gaze darted between the pastor and the crackers, and she let him touch her head as she munched. Even Cat noticed how kind his touch was.

The little girl now stood in front of her, and this time Candy really took in everything about her, from her pale, dirty face to her light blue eyes, which were filled with an emptiness Candy had never seen before in the eyes of a child. She knew there was a mystery about this child that would haunt her when she walked out the door.

Chapter 5

"Where have you been?" Neil called out as Candy shut the door of his SUV. Though she was the only one who really drove the car, it was in his name. She had decided to park in front of the large estate instead of the back, and the front door had flown open when she started up the driveway. She was late, she knew. Dinner had been scheduled for an hour ago.

Neil had to be worried. She had forgotten to charge her cell phone after the morning's drama with Maria, and she had left the house without a word to her husband, hoping she could get away and just think. When she found herself back at the orphanage, all thoughts of Neil and his needs had taken a backseat to the little girl named Cat, who had made a lasting impression on Candy. She'd thought of nothing else but that haunting look. She knew there was a brightness buried deep down in her soul, but why wouldn't she talk? None of it made sense.

She tucked the keys into her purse when Becky and Rodney appeared in the doorway.

"Everything okay, Candy?" Becky asked. She was a

kind, plump woman with whom Candy still struggled to have any kind of mother-daughter relationship. Candy had never had a mother or understood what it was to be part of a family with a bond as strong as the Friessen's. Becky was a wonderful woman, and Rodney … well, what could she say about the head of the Friessen clan? He was an amazing man, and their relationship was one of mutual respect. With an estate as large as this one, they only saw each other for dinner and the odd breakfast, though, so it wasn't as if they were underfoot or crowding in on Candy and Neil.

"Sorry, I lost track of time," she said.

Neil looked a little worse for wear, as if he'd been pulling his hair out worrying about her. "I called a dozen times. I was about to send out a search party for you," he said.

She knew he was exaggerating, sort of—but she also knew he wouldn't hesitate to hire someone to look for her. "I forgot to charge my cell phone," she said. "I didn't realize that it was dead until I went to call you. I'm sorry." She touched his chest and leaned up, erasing all his tension and aggravation in a hard, hurried kiss. His hands went to her shoulders, holding her a bit, and he shut his eyes as if he needed to pull himself together.

"You scared me," he said. "Don't do that again, okay?" He slid his arm around her, pulling her closer and walking her into the house. She loved being this close to Neil, being with him this way. The way he held her made her feel important and needed.

"We haven't eaten dinner yet. Ana left it in the oven for us," Becky added after Neil closed the front door.

"You shouldn't have waited for me," Candy said.

"Don't be silly. It didn't hurt us any to wait, and

besides, we were all starting to worry. We didn't know where you were," Becky said.

"Yeah, where were you?" Neil asked as they started into the dining room. Candy hesitated, not wanting to share the orphanage with Rodney and Becky. Maybe that was what Neil picked up on. "Candy, what's going on?"

"Rodney, give me a hand in the kitchen," Becky said as she glanced between the two, going so far as to reach for Rodney's hand. "Come on. Ana is gone for the night, so she and Carlos aren't here to wait on us hand and foot."

Candy knew her mother-in-law was a smart lady. She never interfered, knowing when to give both her and Neil space. That was just another one of the wonderful qualities of Becky Friessen. Candy wanted to smile as she listened to Rodney grumble as he followed Becky into the kitchen, but she put her hands on the back of a dining room chair and held tight, sucking on her bottom lip, knowing full well her husband was watching her. When she looked up, he was frowning.

"I was at an orphanage," she said, rubbing the chair back with her fingers.

Neil was watching her intently, his arms crossed. He started to say something but instead let out a breath. "Why?" he finally asked. When she didn't answer, mainly because she couldn't figure out what to say, he gestured and said, "Listen, we've already decided we're not adopting, Candy. We've got a surrogate, and she's agreed to all the terms of the agreement. In fact, she met with my lawyer and signed the contract just over an hour ago. It's settled."

She couldn't believe it. Had he not heard one word she'd said to him this morning? Hadn't he promised her he wouldn't go ahead and make decisions of this magnitude without her? She actually found herself searching her memory to see whether, in fact, she had agreed. "Neil, what the hell are you doing, going ahead and agreeing to this? When I left here, this wasn't a done deal, and now it's signed? Where do I fit in to this?"

She could hear Rodney and Becky as they filed into the dining room, carrying pots and dishes and setting them on the table. At this point, she was too angry to care whether they heard her or not. This was crazy, all of it. Her father-in-law was watching her. She could feel the heat of his gaze, and when she looked over, he was taking in both her and Neil.

"You know what? I'm not hungry," Candy said. "If you'll excuse me …" She stepped around Neil. When he went to touch her, she pulled away.

"Candy, stop. This is crazy, you acting like this," he snapped, but she didn't stop. She kept going up the stairs into their bedroom and shut the door.

Chapter 6

She had just dried herself off after soaking in the bathtub for almost half an hour when the door clicked open.

"Candy?" she heard Neil call out. Something clattered, and then there was a rustling.

She pulled on a pink silk housecoat that fit like a second skin and tied the belt as she wandered into the dressing area. Neil appeared around the corner. She was so lost in thought that she hadn't heard him come in. His eyes flared as they always did when he took in the silk that hugged her every curve. It was a thin material, one that never stayed on her very long before Neil peeled it off. For the first time in a long while, she felt awkward, pressing her hand to her throat and open chest as if trying to cover herself.

Maybe he understood how she was feeling, as he said, "Don't hide yourself from me, Candy." He sighed. "I'm sorry." He seemed tired. He looked away and sighed again. "I brought dinner up for you. You have to eat something."

"Thank you," she said, making no move to touch him.

She wondered if she'd ever get past this feeling. "I can't do this anymore, Neil."

His expression became worried and irritated at the same time, but she knew her husband well enough to know that they were drifting so far apart that neither thought they could reach the other. Neil was on a different journey, one that really didn't include her. How could she get him to understand that doing everything his way wasn't going to work this time, not for something like this?

"Candy, I don't understand what's going on with you. We want a baby. Why are you fighting this?" he asked. She lowered her eyes to the floor and started around him, but he put his hand on her arm. "Hey, don't walk away. You go on and on about me excluding you in our marriage, but isn't that exactly what you're doing?"

Candy took in the love for her in his eyes. He really had powerful eyes. The warm amber could reach inside of her and touch her heart, and she always found herself softening toward him. "That's not what I'm doing," she said. "You're just going ahead and doing things without talking to me again. You promised me you wouldn't." She ran her hand down his arm, unable to hide her sadness. She stepped around him and into the bedroom, taking in the tray he had set on the sofa table: a salad, roasted chicken, asparagus. There was even a bottle of wine and two glasses. "Thank you for bringing dinner up," she whispered. She didn't need to turn around to know he was right there behind her, and she reached for a piece of cucumber on top of the salad and munched, taking in the tang of the balsamic vinaigrette.

Neil's hands slid around her front, flattening over her stomach and pulling her against him. "Stop pushing me away," he said. "I love you." He kissed her cheek, and she couldn't resist his touch. She loved him so much. Being this close to him was the easy part—it always had been. When he held her like this, she often forgot her anger, but he had gone too far this time, she reminded herself again.

"Neil, I love you, but you can't keep doing this," she said. She fought against her body, wanting to lean against Neil and give in to him. She couldn't do that, though, so she wiggled away and faced him, holding her hands out so he'd stay back. "Shutting me out and making decisions this important without me … this is about our baby, Neil, and you're making me feel as if I'm an afterthought. You can't just make a decision and then let me know at some point, thinking I'll somehow be okay with it.

"I'm telling you right now that I'm not okay with any of this. When I left the house today, you had convinced me we were just considering things while Maria looked over your contract, and nothing had been decided—or so I thought, but in the few hours I was gone, you went ahead and signed the contract?" She took another step back when Neil reached for her. She knew he had a way of clouding her thinking, and with something this important, she couldn't just let him have his way.

"Candy, you were gone a long time. I called you because Maria was all in. She had reviewed the contract and agreed to all my terms, but I couldn't get a hold of you. I must have left you three messages."

"You left me three messages and then decided that, because you couldn't get a hold of me, you needed to sign it today? What was the rush, Neil? I need you to explain it to me, because I don't understand." She wrapped her arms around her front, watching him.

"I want a baby, Candy. You know how important this is to me. I don't want to wait any more. You said you wanted a family, so I don't understand why you're hesitating now and picking a fight with me over this gift that's being handed to us! We'll have our baby, so why are you fighting this?" He sat on the bed, frustrated, and lowered his head, running his hands over his short, dark hair and ruffling it.

She didn't know how to make him understand. "Neil, you keep taking away my right to speak, as if I don't have a voice in this. I don't want any more surprises. How do you think this makes me feel, that you have to go and find another woman to give you a child? The fact that I, as your wife, can't give you what you so desperately want?"

He was watching her with steel in his eyes. Then he was on his feet and in front of her, his hands gripping her shoulders, holding her when she tried to move away. He leaned closer to her, and for a minute she thought he was going to shake her. "Candy, are you kidding me? I thought we were past this! That is not your fault. God, I would give anything if I could make it happen, if you could give us a child. But we were dealt a shitty hand, baby, and it's not fair. What I can do is give you a child this way. No child could ask for a better, more loving mother than you! Candy, we can't keep thinking about what could have been. This is where we are, and it's good, so why are you trying to turn this gift of a surrogate into something it's not? I can promise you there'll be no problems. This will be easy, and then you'll hold our baby in your arms. Please, Candy, stop fighting this!" He was holding her face between the palms of his hands, and the way he looked at her made her want to give in to him, to just say yes.

She started to say something, but doubt rushed back in. Was she creating a problem that wasn't there? After all, Neil always went ahead and did things like this. He always made decisions without talking to her. That was who he was, and if she allowed this to come between them ... well, she just didn't want that. Neil Friessen was the love of her life, so she found it easy to lean into his hand. Breathing in the scent of him made her want to taste him, to touch him.

He rubbed his nose against hers. His lips teased her, brushing across hers before he kissed her deeply, a hard, bruising, claiming kiss as his tongue touched hers, his hands down her back, pulling her tight against him, not letting her go—not that she could step away from him now. Touching him, kissing him, feeling him inside her were all things that she needed, and she couldn't stop now.

Neil hooked his hands in her housecoat, opening it and slipping it off her shoulders in one move, allowing it to fall to the floor. She stood before him, letting him run his hands over her skin, which already felt branded by him. She had her arms around his neck, her hands in his hair, trying to get closer. Her breasts rubbed against his shirt. She wanted to feel his chest, to feel his weight on her. She automatically reached for the buttons, her hands shaking as he lifted her and climbed onto the bed, pressing her into the mattress. Her fingers fumbled and pulled, and he finally covered her hands with his, breaking the kiss as he pulled away and ripped off his shirt.

"Neil," she whispered, reaching for him. He quickly shed the rest of his clothes, climbing on the bed as she slid her legs open. With a hand on her thighs, he pressed them wider, sliding his hand up higher and around her waist, skimming her breasts as he leaned over, his face so close. He watched her as he entered her, and she took all of him.

It was at times like this, when the world was so far away, that she believed nothing could come between them. It was just them, Candy and Neil, in this moment: touching him, feeling him, loving him. There was nothing soft and gentle with Neil now. It was claiming, and with every movement in the power of his hips as he watched her, she knew she truly belonged to him.

After, she laid on her side, spooned against him, his hand over her stomach, all his lean hardness pressed up against her. She was breathing deeply but was very much awake. He traced his fingers over her hip and then lower, and not a word passed between them as he took her again. It was hard and possessive, bordering on pure, raw need.

"Are you okay?" he mumbled, his chin resting on top of her head.

She exhaled again. "Yeah," she said, allowing his hand to run over and link with hers. She squeezed, not wanting to let him go.

"I didn't hurt you?" he asked, running his hand over her breast.

She didn't think she could answer, so she shook her head. As she reached back, sliding her hand over his naked buttocks, she felt his hardness grow again for her. He rolled her onto her back and was above her, between her thighs, holding himself up. The look in his eyes was pure animal need—nothing gentle, nothing soft. She allowed him to settle between her legs again, and his gaze took in her desire for him. There were no words now. He leaned in and kissed her deeply, letting her know that tonight was about them, just the two of them, and his need for her.

Chapter 7

Candy rinsed the shampoo from her hair. She was less tired than expected, seeing as Neil hadn't allowed her more than a few minutes of sleep the night before. He spent the night loving her and exploring her body over and over. She could still feel him inside her, and she couldn't remember ever having felt so claimed by him. Where had he gotten his stamina? By morning, when he took her for the last time, she wondered whether she'd be able to walk. It had been hard and fast, as if he had been trying to remind her to whom she belonged. She wondered what had gotten into him. Sex with Neil was always great, but last night it had been off the charts. They'd said nothing to each other between kissing, touching, and caressing, and it had seemed, at times, that he was trying to memorize the taste of her.

"Candy," Neil said. He was already dressed and pulling open the shower door, and he looked at her with a gleam in his eyes, pleased with what he saw. "Breakfast is ready. We need to talk."

What now? Maybe she should be grateful he was talking, at least. She shut off the shower, and he wrapped her in a towel as she stepped out and then dried her hair with another as he stood behind her.

"My lawyer just called," he said. "We need to go in and sign the agreement, but I don't want you to feel that I've cut you out. That was never my intention. I need you to be comfortable with the entire process of this surrogacy. I haven't signed the agreement yet. It was just Maria who signed it yesterday." He took a breath, and she could feel how close he was. "You need to sign it, as well."

She didn't expect that. Maybe he realized how startled she was, as he put his hands on her shoulders as she stared in the steamed mirror. She could make out his blurred figure as he leaned down and kissed her cheek, and she covered his hand with hers, wondering if she had finally gotten through to him, making him understand her need to be included in his decisions. She turned in his arms and put her hands to his face, then reached up on her tiptoes and kissed him.

"Mmm," he murmured as he kissed her back. When he pulled away, she didn't miss the heat lingering in his eyes. He wanted her, and she felt connected to him in a way that was deep and meaningful. Maybe it would be okay. "If you keep it up, we're going to end up back in bed, and you surely won't be walking today," he said. "Besides, you need to get dressed. We have to get going." He kissed her again and this time left her in the bathroom to finish getting ready.

Forty minutes later, after a quick breakfast, Candy was in the passenger side of Neil's black Range Rover, dressed in a cream sundress and low sandals, her long hair tied back in a simple ponytail.

She felt content and well loved for the first time in a long while, and she wanted to share everything with her husband. "I've been visiting an orphanage on the island," she said.

She watched Neil as he darted his gaze from the road to her. His shades covered his eyes so she couldn't really tell what he was thinking. His expression was curious, neutral. She wasn't really sure, but, for a moment, she wondered whether he was even interested.

"Yes, you mentioned that last night," he said, shifting his gaze back to the road.

Candy didn't know what to say. For a minute, she had to look away. She couldn't help feeling hurt that he didn't want to know more about what she'd been doing. Neil wasn't self-centered, but it really felt like their marriage was all about him, and anything about her—her thoughts, her feelings, her passions—took a backseat. Maybe it had always been that way, and she'd just never seen it.

"So your lawyer's going to walk us through this entire process?" She circled her hand nervously in front of her and then cleared her throat.

"I'm bothered that you went to an orphanage, Candy. To see that ..." He stopped and then sighed, glancing at her again. "You're too sensitive. It had to bother you to see all those innocent faces."

She stared at Neil, not knowing what to say. There were times when he surprised the hell out of her. "I stopped in after we got back from your cousin's, looking for an option to adopt," she began. "There are so many children looking for a home. They have no babies, but they have so many young children—I saw their need and I just had to help."

She could feel the way he watched her as he pulled into the parking lot behind a two-story building. He shut off the engine and turned in his seat, the leather rustling as he rested his arm over the steering wheel.

"I bought them beds," she said, wondering whether he'd be angry at her for spending the money and not saying anything. "I'm sorry I didn't say anything or ask you if it was okay, but they're over capacity. Children sleep on blankets on concrete floors, others crowded on beds that belong in a dump—"

"Candy, you don't need to ask me if you can spend money. You never spend a dime. I can't even get you to go out and buy new shoes or a dress—anything. If you think I didn't notice the charge, I did. I meant to ask you, but this all came up." He gestured to the building, and she wondered whether he meant the surrogate or the lawyer. He reached across the seat and squeezed her hand. "Let's go."

He opened his door, and she met him around the front of the vehicle, where he reached for her hand and held it as they walked into his lawyer's office.

Les Feldman was tall and slender, with thin white hair and deep blue eyes. He was in his sixties, having retired from his fast-tracked corporate career in Cleveland ten years earlier. Neil had said that his lawyer had, at times, bordered on the shady side with some of his clients, but he had made a pile of money and wanted the easy life now. Neil was one of just a few clients he represented down in Cancun.

"Candy and Neil, great to see you," Les said. He reached out and shook Neil's hand but kissed Candy on the cheek. She'd never get used to that, and it felt almost as if he was crossing the line. She wondered why Neil always seemed okay with his lawyer touching her as he did. With any other man, she knew he would have lost it. Maybe it was something about their relationship, their friendship … whatever it was. She knew they were close.

He pulled out a file from the desk where his secretary

usually sat, but the office was empty. She looked around and then to Neil, who accepted some papers that Les handed him.

"Here is the original that Maria signed. Her mother was with her yesterday. Once you sign"—Les glanced over at Candy—"both of you, we can make arrangements for her accommodations, and then there's the counseling. We have a psychologist lined up for her, and it would be best if you two went, as well."

Candy looked to Neil, puzzled by the mention of accommodations. She needed to find out more about the counseling, too. Neil was busy reading something, and then, without looking at Candy, he put his hand on her back as they followed Les into his office.

"So she had no questions, and she agreed to my terms?" Neil asked. Les shut the door behind them and walked around the desk to sit in his chair. Neil pulled a chair out for Candy and then sat in the other. He leaned back, still reading the legalese, then put his finger on the dip below his lower lip; the spot she loved to kiss.

He flicked his gaze to her and leaned closer, then set the paper on the desk and reached for the pen. When he scribbled his name, it was completely unreadable, but it was his signature. He handed her the pen. "You need to sign right here, honey," he said.

She met his gaze. Les was watching her, peering over the top of his glasses. Did he have any idea how her husband was controlling things, especially this entire surrogacy? Candy gripped the pen and touched her tongue to her lower lip. She set the pen down on the desk, picked up the papers, and leaned back in the chair, crossing one leg over the other.

"What are you doing?" Neil asked. She could see the glance exchanged between him and his lawyer, and she realized Les had expected her to just sign the paper. Well, he needed a reality check.

She held the papers and glanced over at her husband. "I'm going to read this over before I sign my name," she said. She glanced over at Les. "You don't mind, do you, if I actually read what I'm signing?"

She didn't wait for him or Neil to answer—but she didn't miss the heaviness in her husband's breathing as he leaned back in his chair and waited.

Chapter 8

She was sitting in the passenger side of the Range Rover beside a very annoyed Neil, who'd said only two words to her: "Let's go." That had been after she'd made him wait for forty minutes while she read the document not once, but three times, mainly because she kept stumbling over the legalese and had to reread the passages to make sense of them. For the first time, she'd felt stupid sitting next to her smart, educated husband, who could have written this up himself. Even though she knew he was furious with her for taking so long, she just couldn't ask him to translate it for her.

The drive home seemed endless and tense—which, of course, she was partly responsible for. She couldn't get over how he felt he knew what was best for her. He had told her they would read over the documents together, but it was almost as if, since he had read them, he honestly believed she didn't need to. Well, he was wrong!

Neil took the last turn home a little fast and drove up the driveway around the side of the house, skidding to a stop by the garage. She put her hand on the dashboard, the shoulder strap digging into her shoulder. So he was mad, too. She unbuckled her seat belt and opened the door before he could turn the engine off, carrying her cloth purse and starting toward the house, where Rodney and Becky were lounging out back by the pool.

"So, tell me, how did it go this morning?" Becky called out, sounding quite pleased. Of course she knew, and Candy would bet Becky knew more of the details than she did.

"Ask your son," Candy said. She kept walking but didn't miss the look of shock on her mother-in-law's face. She was in the back door and had just closed it when she heard Neil speaking with his mother. She couldn't make out his words, but she wasn't really interested in sitting around and eavesdropping. She headed upstairs to their room, sliding the zipper of her dress down and stepping out of it, leaving it in a heap on the floor as she kicked off the silver strappy sandals that Neil had bought for her. She strode into the closet and pulled on a pair of worn jeans and an older t-shirt; she was sitting on the bed and slipping on a pair of socks just as the bedroom door opened and Neil walked in.

His eyes went right to her dress (in a heap on the floor) and her shoes (kicked in the corner). Candy didn't say a word as she got up, went into the closet, and looked over the fancy riding boots Neil had bought her. She had never worn them, instead opting for her old ankle-high boots, the soles of which had been re-stitched a couple of times. Now, she reached for her sneakers and shoved them on her feet. She didn't need to turn around to know her husband was standing in the doorway of the closet, watching her. He was mad, of course. Les had had another appointment, and Candy had been responsible for making his next client wait.

She pulled out the elastic holding her hair back and shook her head. She took two steps and then stopped, taking in Neil and the way he narrowed his eyes. Oh, he was mad, all right. She swallowed and then linked her hands in front of her, just watching him right back. She wasn't caving, not this time. "Excuse me," she said as she started past him.

Neil put his hand on her arm and stopped her. "Just a minute," he said. "I need to know, what's going on with you?"

She glanced up at him slowly. She couldn't believe how he was twisting this. "Me, are you kidding? You said we were going to your lawyer's to read over the agreement so I could understand everything before I signed."

He had the nerve to actually glance up at the ceiling as if she were testing his patience.

"Oh, I see!" she snapped. "I'm supposed to blindly trust you, here. You read, and I be the good little wifey and sign on the dotted line exactly where you tell me. Ask no questions, hmm?" She tilted her head and narrowed her eyes. "No." She slapped his hand away and started around him.

"Are you telling me that, after everything we've been through, you don't trust me?" he asked.

She stopped in their bedroom and bent over to pick up the dress, shaking it out and tossing it on the bed. "Of course I trust you, but I'm stunned, Neil. Did you think I was just going to sign a legal document without reading it? No, wait. Don't answer that, because I already know what you're going to say." She swept her hand in the air. "I don't know why you're so upset, anyway. I signed your damn contract." She started to the door.

"Where are you going?" he asked, though it was more like a demand.

"Somewhere that I'm needed," she replied.

Chapter 9

"You can't just turn her over to the authorities! Stall them—do something," Candy begged Pastor Mendoza, who seemed so tired in his office at the orphanage.

"I don't know if I can. Rosita reported the little girl as retarded. They don't usually respond like this, but they're coming for her. We are over capacity, or I don't think they'd have cared."

"You mean Rosita, that woman who was here looking after Cat, scaring her to death … she's responsible for this?"

He inclined his head. His dark hair was tangled and sticking up, and she wondered whether he'd even brushed it today. Probably not. He was so much the opposite of her husband.

Candy put both of her hands on his desk. "She isn't *retarded*," she snapped.

Pastor Mendoza leaned forward and seemed to be considering what to say as he stood up. "Candy, we don't know what, except there is something wrong with that child. She needs more than we can give her. She scares the other children, and she was almost run down by the truck that comes in to bring supplies. It blasted its horn, and she didn't respond. She could have been killed, but it's not just that—"

"I looked into her eyes, and what I see is a child everyone has cast aside," Candy said, cutting the pastor off. "No one has given that poor child even one ounce of sympathy. She needs kindness, she needs love; not to be tossed into some facility where she'll never be seen again. You and I both know how bad those places are. They're tied to the walls in wheelchairs, the floors are stained with urine and feces, they scream in agony and no one hears them … You'd be kinder to put a gun to her head and pull the trigger! We could do that for an animal, but not for a child. What has this world come to?" She sighed. "Please, just let me try something," she finally said.

His dark eyes widened with a flash of anger. "What are you going to try that I haven't? Even Doctor Ortega has said there was nothing that could be done."

"That old man can't even be considered a doctor. He's a butcher and has been practicing his quack medicine since before I was born," she snapped. The pastor looked away, as if he was shutting her out. Insulting someone who often helped him wasn't the way to go, she knew that. "I'm sorry," she said. "Please just give me some time to do something."

"What are you going to do?"

"I'm going to find her the right help, the kind of help that only money can buy."

He seemed to consider something as he stared at her, his hand gripping his chin. "You have one day. That's all I can give you. I won't be able to hold them off longer than that."

"Thank you," Candy said. She put her hand over her heart, taking a breath, wondering where to start. Her cell phone started ringing. "Excuse me a second, Pastor." She reached into her purse with every intention of letting the call go to voicemail when she saw her husband's name flash on the screen. She didn't have the energy to go another round with him, but it was more out of duty than anything else that she hit *Talk*. "Neil, I can't speak with you right now."

"Candy, I thought you would want to know we're going over to the IVF clinic this afternoon to start the procedure. I thought you would want to be here," he said.

She could feel the wall between them as he spoke, and she touched her head, feeling as if her husband was moving in a different direction than she was. "I didn't know it was going to start now. I just signed the agreement. How can you arrange things this quickly?" She turned her back on the pastor when his expression became concerned.

Neil sighed. "Les made some calls, got it all arranged as soon as we left. Why wait? We want this, so let's make it happen. We've waited a long time for a baby, a child of our own." He groaned on the other end. "Candy, come on. Would you please just come, baby? You can't not be here. This is too important."

She rubbed her forehead, thinking. She needed to figure out what to do for Cat. "When is it?"

"Now. Just tell me where you are, and I'll come and get you."

She gritted her teeth. This could start another fight. "No, I'll meet you there. Just tell me where to go."

"Candy, where are you?" he demanded.

She knew she was provoking all his worries. For the first time, his overprotective male side was making her feel anything but protected and cherished. "At the orphanage."

"Candy, why?" he snapped. She could hear his frustration, and she couldn't believe that Neil, of all people, could be so cold.

"Because I'm needed here!"

"Oh my God, Candy, are you serious? You're needed *here*, and soon you're going to have a baby who'll need you. Which orphanage are you at?"

"Casa Perdido," she said, waiting for him to say something else to make her feel inadequate.

Instead, all he said was "I'll be there in ten. Wait for me inside." Then he hung up.

Chapter 10

"Would you like this hairbrush? I could brush your hair for you," Candy said. She was sitting cross legged on the floor in the room where Cat was, wearing the same dirty dress she had worn the day before. When she had walked in, Rosita, the spiteful woman with the bruise on her face from where Cat had socked her, met Candy with a glare that seemed to shoot fire, she was so angry.

Cat was staring at the brush Candy was holding, and she reached out and ran her fingers over the bristles. She looked up at Candy, her hair tangled and dirty. The girl looked untamed, as if she did belong in an institution. No one could get her cleaned up without her going ballistic.

"She doesn't understand you," Rosita said. "You're wasting your time on that one when there are so many others out there that need your help." She was standing over her, staring at Cat as if she was nothing.

"Well, then, you should go help them. I'll stay with Cat."

"Candy," came a voice from the doorway. It was Neil,

his sunglasses dangling between his fingers as he took in the bare skeleton of a room. She knew that he didn't miss much, and she could also tell he wasn't happy, though she didn't even want to guess why. At this point, he could have been angry about any number of things: she'd kept him waiting, he was still mad about this morning, or, quite possibly, he just didn't want her to be at the orphanage.

"Just give me a minute, Neil. I want to brush Cat's hair," she said. She just couldn't bear leaving and walking out the door, leaving the child in that condition. With Rosita hovering the way she was, Candy was worried about what the woman would do to Cat after she left. "Cat, I'm just going to brush your hair. I'll be really gentle."

She lifted the brush and touched the little girl's head, and Cat whipped out her hand and smacked her. She started mewing, an awful sound, lashing out and catching Candy in the eye and face.

"Stop it!" Neil shouted. He grabbed Cat and held her arms, pinning them to her sides.

Cat was now making an inconsolable sound, and Candy felt a sting on her lip. She brushed her hand over it, seeing the blood as she pulled it away.

"You okay?" Neil asked. He was still holding Cat as the pastor hurried in.

"What happened?" he said, taking in Candy and Cat, whom Neil was still holding.

"This girl hit Candy when she tried to brush her hair," Neil said.

The pastor reached for Cat and somehow managed to calm her down.

"It was my fault," Candy said. "I was hurrying. She was just beginning to trust me, and I didn't want to leave with her looking like this."

The pastor looked up at Rosita, who was in the background, shaking her head, taking it all in. "That will be all, Rosita," he said. "I think you are needed in the kitchen."

Thankfully, the woman left.

"Candy, you need to go with your husband," Rafael said as he stood up, leaving Cat to move into the corner, where she sat in a huddle.

"I don't want to leave right now," Candy said. She was panicking over what had happened. If something happened to Cat when she left, she knew she'd never forgive herself.

Neil stepped closer and slid his hand on Candy's cheek, dabbing at her lip. "Would someone please fill me in on what's going on here?" he said, but he didn't look at the pastor when he asked. Neil Friessen was staring at his wife.

Chapter 11

Neil leaned against the pastor's desk. Candy could see how he was taking in everything about the orphanage that she had been visiting for weeks, ever since they'd returned from Montana. His expression told her everything he was thinking. At least she now had all of his attention. He listened when she told him about Cat and how Rosita had gone to the authorities, and she knew Neil understood the situation. After seeing the little girl, he must have realized how easy it would be for the authorities to just shove her into an institution.

Neil shook his head, his hand to his chin. She could tell his heart was open, but then, whose wouldn't be, after taking in that tiny child and her situation? By the softness in his eyes when they connected with hers, she knew he understood—maybe better than she did—what a death sentence it would be for Cat if the authorities got a hold of her and locked her away. He knew what really went on behind the closed doors of the institutions. After all, Mexico had done little to improve conditions for disabled people who had no one to look after them. They were the lost souls, those without a voice. No one would notice them gone. No one would care.

He shook his head again and sighed, taking in Candy and then Pastor Mendoza, who was wearing ripped jeans and a worn t-shirt. He stood up and pulled out his wallet, lifting out a wad of cash and tossing it on the desk. "I'll have a check brought over, as well. It's all I can do right now, but there's enough cash there to see that the girl gets some help. Hire someone to be with her, and I'll make a call to my lawyer to see that she stays here." He then held out his hand to Candy. "We need to go," he said.

She couldn't believe it. "Neil, what about Cat?" she said. How could he leave now, after seeing Cat and the help she needed?

"There's nothing else we can do for her right now, and we have an appointment—or have you forgotten already? I'm here to pick you up."

"Maybe I should follow you. I drove, remember?"

He just shook his head. "Give me the keys," he said. When she did, he tossed them on the pastor's desk. "I'll send someone for my wife's SUV," he told him. "Candy, let's go."

Candy looked to Pastor Mendoza to say something, but he fingered the cash Neil had tossed and looked at them both. "Mister Friessen, you're very generous," he said. "This will go a long way to help the children here."

"Hire someone for the little girl with that money," Neil said as he jabbed a finger toward the pastor, taking Candy's hand.

"Her name is Cat, Neil," she said.

He glanced her way, distracted. "For Cat, Pastor. That money is for her. Whatever else you need; let me know," he said. He started out of the small office into the narrow concrete hallway. It was dingy and plain, with cracks in the wall, and Candy could smell the mold even though the women who volunteered here scrubbed and cleaned what they could.

"Neil, wait," she said.

He didn't stop, pulling her out of the orphanage by the hand. She had to practically jog to keep up with him, he was moving so fast. He opened the passenger door of his fancy Range Rover. "Get in," he said sharply. When she climbed in, he shut the door behind her and walked around the front of the vehicle, shoving his shades on and climbing behind the wheel. He said nothing to her as he backed out and pulled into the busy traffic, driving faster than usual.

"Why didn't you tell me what was going on?" he finally said. "You've been sneaking off for weeks to this place, to this part of town. I don't want you down here! What you've been doing is far different than just visiting an orphanage."

He was mad, all right, weaving around cars and braking fast whenever someone cut him off. He swore under his breath. He never got irritated, not like this.

"Honestly, Neil, I really didn't think you wanted to know," she said. "Thank you for helping Cat, though. She has no one."

He shook his head but didn't look at her. "What kind of monster do you think I am? Of course I care. Do you think I like seeing children treated like that? Of course I'd help her. I left enough money so that the pastor can hire someone to come in and do what's needed for her."

"I'm going back to help her, Neil."

"No," Neil snapped. "Take a look at what she did to your face. She's beyond your help. She needs someone who knows how to look after a child like her."

She blanched as if he'd slapped her. It felt like he had,

anyway. "If I'm not capable of helping Cat, how am I capable of looking after a baby?" she said softly, the words aching as they passed her lips.

"Oh, geez, Candy, seriously?" He pulled into a parking spot at the medical clinic, a newer building with a big green sign out front. He shut off the engine and pulled the keys from the ignition, jiggling them in his hand as he glanced at Candy with a look bordering on exasperation. It seemed as if he didn't even know how to talk to her.

She was at the same point, and she realized, as she watched him climb out and walk around his Range Rover, that whatever journey they were on, they had somehow taken different paths. It hurt to realize that whatever she did and whatever she said, Neil had already turned away and was moving further down the river, pursuing his own goals and objectives. She wondered now if any of that included her.

Chapter 12

The waiting room at the fertility clinic held half a dozen people. The room was shaped in an L, with white walls, magazines on coffee tables, and cloth-covered chairs. A few expensive pieces of artwork were framed and placed here and there on the walls. It was nice, the kind of place you knew, right away, that you had to have money to enter. Maybe that was why Candy felt a little underdressed in her worn jeans. She was also self-conscious about how her face looked. She'd stopped in the bathroom on the way in to examine herself in the mirror: There was a red mark at the corner of her eye that anyone would notice, and her lip was cut and a little swollen.

Everyone probably thought her husband was beating her or something. Even the nurse behind the desk had been unable to hide her surprise when she took in Candy's face.

Of course Neil, being Neil, frowned and pulled her aside by the door. "You have any makeup in that purse of yours?"

Candy just shook her head. "No," she said.

"Great. Just great, Candy."

She sat beside him. She was tempted to move over one seat, but she had to force herself not to go there, reminding herself that it would only make the situation worse. It would definitely fuel the suspicions going through the minds of the couples in the waiting room—or maybe she was just being paranoid because of the odd glances she was getting.

"Can you fill me in, Neil?" she said, clasping her hands beside him. She wondered if he understood how uncomfortable she was. "What's going to happen now?"

"I supply a donation, the egg is fertilized, and then it's done" was all he said before the nurse stood up and called out, "Mister Friessen?"

Neil didn't even look her way as he got up and followed the nurse through a door, leaving her there alone. What surprised her more than anything, after what they'd been through, was that he didn't ask her to go with him. They'd never discussed this part … the donation. What would happen with Maria? She wanted details, and no one was providing them. For a moment, she felt as if Neil was cheating on her, which made absolutely no sense. At the same time, she sat there and then fumbled for a magazine, wondering why she was here. Maybe she was just supposed to sit by as a doting wife. That was one thing about Neil; he did like to know where she was.

She flipped a page in a beauty magazine that she really had no interest in when the door opened and two chatting women strode in—Carmen and Maria. It was an uncomfortable moment, and she hated when the women both stopped, eyes widening as they took her in.

"Oh, nice to see you, Missus Friessen," Maria said, all smiles.

Carmen tilted her head, really taking in Candy's face. "Did something happen?" she asked, a little concerned.

It would be so easy to let them think Neil did this to her. Then maybe they'd go away and she wouldn't have to deal with the two of them. But the moment that thought crossed her mind, she felt ashamed and knew Neil would be furious. "It was an accident, really. I was just volunteering, and … my face got in the way." She stumbled over the last part because she couldn't tell anyone how Cat had hit her. She knew the little girl had been terrified, lashing out to protect herself. She probably thought Candy was going to hurt her. Candy had been so distracted and rushed when Neil appeared that she had tried to hurry, and she knew, better than anyone, that when you were building trust, you couldn't rush.

"Oh," Carmen said. She glanced at her daughter and shooed her to the front desk with a smile. "Go on up there and check in with the nurse."

Candy watched the happy exchange, and Maria waved to her mother before being led through a door, probably to another room. Her heart sank when the door closed. Having Neil and Maria on the other side of the door made it seem like they were together. She knew that was ridiculous, but she now felt completely left out. How could she explain to anyone this hollowness that cut through her chest? She didn't want to sit and wait outside making pleasant conversation with Carmen, a woman that she knew didn't like her. The silence was strained as Carmen sat there, keeping a chair between them, her chin high. She had a pride in her expression that put Candy on edge, and then she reached over and picked up her own magazine, crossing her legs and flipping the pages.

"So, today is the day," Carmen said. She smiled over at Candy, but it never reached her eyes. Having Carmen dislike her this much was hard, but being stuck in the same room with her was worse. Candy couldn't remember ever picking up on someone's negativity toward her this much.

"Excuse me," she said, tossing the magazine on the table when the nurse reappeared at the desk. She wandered up and rested both hands on the counter, leaning over so no one could hear. "Hi, I have a question."

The nurse looked up.

"Are there any pediatricians or really good children's doctors around here?" she asked.

The nurse had long, dark hair tied back in a ponytail. She seemed to consider before nodding. "Well, yes, there are. As you know, some are better than others." She paused as if thinking and then rummaged in a drawer before pulling out a card and handing it to Candy. "Try Doctor Miller. We send a lot of referrals to him. His office is just around the corner in the next building."

Candy clutched the white card, taking in the American name—Jim Miller. "Thank you," she said. She started to turn back to her chair when she felt the burning gaze of Carmen. Frankly, it was creeping her out the way the woman was watching her. She turned back to the nurse. "Do you know how much longer my husband is going to be?"

The nurse actually suppressed a smile. "Some take longer than others."

"I see," she replied. She had to fight the urge to press her hand to her throat to hide her discomfort. "You know what, could you tell my husband I had to step out and I'll be back?"

"Of course I will," the nurse said.

Candy tapped the counter and then strode to the door, offering a polite smile to Carmen before leaving without saying a word. As soon as she shut the door and stood in the empty hallway, she had to fight the urge to sag in relief. She took a deep breath, feeling a hundred-pound weight lift off her shoulders. She read the address on the card and hurried down the outside stairs and into the bright afternoon sun. No matter what Neil thought or said, she wasn't going to go back in there and sit. She didn't belong, and being a third wheel was not something Candy was comfortable with.

She hurried around the corner, flitting between tourists and residents walking down both sides of the street. She stopped when she spotted the small sign to the doctor's office and opened the door, stepping into a crowded waiting area. One child was crying, and there were parents sitting there, waiting with other children. A man stood behind the counter, a stethoscope draped around his neck. He had short, light hair and a tanned face spattered with freckles. He glanced up with bright blue eyes. He had a handsome, distracted face.

"Can I help you?" he asked as he stood up from where he was leaning, pocketing the pen he had been writing with. Before she could answer, he gestured over her head to someone. "Freddy, outside with that," he said. "You know better."

She nearly jumped when a gangly teenager bounced a basketball behind her before darting through the door and outside. The doctor glanced back at her, and she could tell she might lose his attention pretty quickly when a nurse appeared at his side and handed him a file. "Excuse me, I'm wondering if I could speak with Doctor Miller for a moment," she said, clutching her purse.

The blond man said something to the nurse and let out a weary sigh. "Yeah, that's me. If you need an appointment, we're booked up for the day, but you can talk to the nurse and she'll pencil you in." He was about to walk away.

"My name is Candy Friessen, and I just need a moment. It's about a little girl at the orphanage. I just need you to take a look at her, please. I can pay whatever it costs."

He didn't appear to hear her as he held up a file and called out, "Carlito?"

"Please, just five minutes," she pleaded, tapping the counter.

There was a man with a little boy behind her. "Doctor Miller, is it our turn?" he asked.

"It is. You can go on back with Rosa, here," the doctor said, gesturing to a plump, dark-haired lady who then took the man and little boy down a hall. "Two minutes is all I can give you. I have a number of patients today, as you can see."

"I'm sorry, I know you're busy, but there's a little girl at the orphanage—she's maybe four or five, and she doesn't talk or even respond when she's asked to do something. She hit me when I tried to brush her hair, but I think she thought I was going to hurt her." She started walking with the doctor down the hall when he gestured for her to go with him. His eyes were amazing, and she could see the compassion in them even though he didn't say anything. She knew she needed to talk faster. "She was found eating out of garbage cans. The authorities found out and now want to put her in a facility for the disabled and insane."

He shook his head, and she didn't miss his disgust. "What do you want me to do, though?" he asked. "If she is mentally challenged, what can I do for her?"

"Please, all I ask is for you to take a look at her. I know she's not crazy. There was something there when she looked at me, I could see it. She's smart, but there's something wrong. I can't reach her, and I don't know why. Please, I'll pay anything. All I'm asking is for you to take a look at her." She knew she was begging, and maybe he picked up on her desperation, as he stopped and groaned, wiping his tired face.

"What's your interest in this girl, one of so many lost children down here? Are you trying to become her guardian, or what is this about?"

That wasn't something she'd even considered, and right now she was really glad Neil wasn't here; he would have shut down that direction of thinking right away. He'd be furious to know she was here, begging this doctor. In fact, she was pleading with him, and she would have gotten down on her knees and begged him if she had to. "I've been helping out down at the orphanage, and I saw how everyone was ready to write her off as if she can't be helped. I don't believe anyone has ever given this child a chance. Please, I'm just asking you to look at her."

He actually swore under his breath and really looked at her. "I'm going to regret this, I can feel it," he said. "What orphanage is she at?"

Candy couldn't stop herself from jumping. "Oh, thank you so much! You don't know what this means." She touched his arm and pulled back, putting her hands together in prayer and touching them to her mouth. "She's at Casa Perdido. When can you see her?"

"After I close up here, I'll go over. No promises, though, Candy," he added as he started down the hall, his hand on his office door. "What's her name?" he asked, more as an afterthought.

"Cat," she said. "Her name is Cat."

Chapter 13

By the time Candy returned to the doctor's office, Neil was in the waiting room, speaking with Carmen. By the dark look on his face, she knew their conversation was all about her. His expression didn't change when he saw her. All he said was "Thanks, Carmen" before starting toward Candy.

Carmen wore a smug expression, and it didn't take someone with a degree to figure out that she seemed to take some joy in Neil's distress with her.

"Where have you been?" he said. Oh, he was mad, all right. "Carmen said you just got up and left without saying anything. No one knew where you were."

"Actually, I spoke with the nurse and asked her to tell you that I had to step out," she said. She resented the way he was talking to her in front of Carmen. Then she noticed Maria coming through the door, her face pink. She blushed as she approached, and Neil immediately changed his demeanor, smiling down at the young woman who now stood at his side. There was a closeness there that bothered Candy, and as she thought about the very personal aspect of this situation, it almost made her sick. Maria could be carrying a child, a part of her husband, inside her right now.

An ache squeezed her chest, making it impossible to breathe, but she stood stoically, wondering if her face would crack from how tightly she was holding her expression.

"All done. We just have to wait now and see if it worked," Neil said. He was beaming at the girl, and Candy couldn't take it any longer.

"Excuse me," she muttered, darting out the door and running down the stairs. She heard footsteps behind her.

"Candy!" Neil shouted, but she didn't stop. As she pushed the door open and ran out into the bright sun, he grabbed her arm. "What's wrong with you?" he asked, though it sounded like an accusation.

This time, she pulled her arm away. "Why did you really want me there, Neil?" Her voice cracked. "To humiliate me?"

She took in his dark expression. He was staring at her as if she'd lost her mind. She knew she wasn't going to be able to explain it to him. Behind them, the door to the clinic opened, and Carmen and Maria stepped through it, hesitating as they stared at Candy and then called out to her husband.

"Thank you, Neil," Maria said. Carmen was smiling brightly.

He turned and stepped away from Candy. "No, thank you, Maria and Carmen. Listen, I'll be in touch. I'll call you tomorrow and see how you're doing ..."

This was way too much for her to be expected to handle. Candy was operating in survival mode as she turned away and started walking. Whatever else Neil said to them, she didn't hear it. She was done.

Chapter 14

"What is wrong with you?" Neil was yelling at her where she sat in the passenger seat of the SUV. He'd never spoken to her this way. After she'd had the emergency hysterectomy, his polite distance had just about killed her, but this situation … well; she didn't know how much more she could take.

"You shouldn't have taken me there, Neil! I didn't belong," she said.

Distantly, she realized they were still sitting in the parking lot outside of the clinic. Nothing had changed, but where could they go from here, really? They were fighting all the time. He didn't listen to her. He couldn't understand how she was feeling, or maybe he was just unwilling to try. What was worse, he had gone ahead and made arrangements for this surrogacy without making sure she understood every aspect. What about the counseling, accommodations for Maria, payment? Would she have to see Maria constantly and watch as her belly began to swell with her husband's child? How much did Neil expect her to endure, just standing by and accepting? They were way past compromising on anything.

"Just drop me off at the orphanage," she said, looking straight ahead through the windshield, her hands clutching her jeans. She swallowed and realized he was still watching her. "Please, Neil, just drop me off." She once again swallowed the ache building in her throat and her chest, but it was expanding to something she would have a hard time holding in. It hurt like nothing she'd experienced before.

"No, I'm not dropping you off, Candy. You're my wife, we're going home. No more orphanage. I should have figured out this was what had you so distracted, why you're acting so oddly. We just had our surrogate inseminated today! Our baby could've already been created, growing inside her. We should be celebrating and counting the days until she can take her pregnancy test!" he shouted. He was getting really loud, though he never yelled at her, not like this. He loved her, she told herself. He was strong minded and strong willed, but he had always worried about how she felt about things—until now.

Neil slammed his hand against the steering wheel. Before he could start the engine, she choked on a sob and opened the door, unclipping her seat belt and slipping out before he could stop her.

"Get back in the vehicle, Candy," he said.

This time, she couldn't stop the tears from sliding down her cheeks. She didn't try to wipe them away as she stared at the fierceness in Neil's expression, as if he were losing control of his temper or were about to leave her on her ass and walk away. She didn't know which, so she glanced away and swiped at her face.

"I think we need some space for a bit," she said. "Go home, Neil. I'll see you later." She didn't wait for him to say anything as she shut her door. She half expected him to climb out after her and go all caveman, dragging her back in.

What she didn't expect was for him to start the engine and drive away. Even though it was exactly what she'd asked of him, she'd never believed he would really do it.

Chapter 15

"You shouldn't be here, Candy. You should go home to your husband," Pastor Mendoza said to her after she returned to the orphanage, having walked the entire way. She wondered whether Neil would have been furious that she hadn't taken a cab, but the fact was that she wanted to clear her head. It wasn't that it was a long walk, but she really needed a moment to toss through her mind everything that had brought both her and Neil to this point.

Could she have done things differently? Had she over-reacted? Possibly. There were a lot of what-ifs. The problem was that she didn't want this surrogacy. There was something about the whole procedure that made her uneasy, and the mess they were in was partly her fault for not standing her ground and telling Neil how she felt right from the beginning.

Candy was now sitting on the floor with Cat, who was playing with a doll she had picked up at a tourist market on the way here. She'd used Neil's credit card. There had been something about the doll that she thought Cat would love, and when she put the doll in front of the girl, she had reached out and taken it, holding on as if her life depended on it. When her light eyes reached out to Candy, she realized she'd made her first connection with this child.

"No, Pastor, I'm not leaving. The doctor said he would come, and I believe he will, after he finishes at his clinic. It can't be much longer."

"It's dinnertime, Candy. The children need to eat."

"And Cat, do you feed her with the other children?" Candy asked as the little girl moved closer to her. Her little body leaned against Candy, her doll clutched in the crook of her arm. Candy glanced down, almost scared to move. She couldn't believe it, and she looked up at the pastor, who was taking everything in.

There was a tap on the outer wall. Candy recognized Doctor Miller: lean, good looking, his blond hair ruffled from a long day. He carried a brown doctor's bag and strode in, his gaze landing on Candy and the little girl beside her. "Jim Miller," he said, reaching out his hand to the pastor. "You must be …"

"Pastor Mendoza. Please, call me Rafael," he said. "You're the doctor Candy told me was coming for our Cat?"

"Yes, Candy was quite convincing. I didn't believe she'd have let me have any peace or get on with my day if I didn't agree to come," he said with a wry smile. "So tell me about this little girl. This is Cat?" He gestured to the girl leaning against Candy now as he moved closer.

She wanted to reach around her and touch her, to hold her. She was worried Cat would freak out. She didn't want to scare her.

"Has she seen a doctor yet?" Jim asked, squatting down

in front of them. He set his bag down and studied the little girl.

"Yes," she replied. "Doctor Ortega—that quack."

"Candy, you're not being fair," Rafael interrupted. "He's not a quack. He donates his time for free."

"If he was any good, he wouldn't have said she was retarded," Candy snapped back.

Jim didn't say a word as he shone a light down on Cat, flicking it on and off. She blinked and looked up. "A doctor diagnosed her as intellectually disabled?" he asked.

Candy couldn't tell what he was thinking. "Yes," she replied before the pastor could say one more thing about it.

"Well, she's not," Jim stated. He was very matter of fact and pulled out an instrument from his bag. "Has she always been this unresponsive?"

"She doesn't talk or respond to us. It's as if she doesn't understand anything we're saying," the pastor added as the doctor flashed the light in front of the little girl's face. She reached out for it, and he kept talking to her, asking her to turn her head. She didn't respond, though.

"I need to look in her ears," he said. "Hold her head, Candy."

The doctor started to insert the probe in Cat's ear after brushing back her hair, and of course she started to wiggle around and claw at Candy's arm.

"It's all right, Cat," she murmured. "Sit still. It won't hurt at all."

The little girl didn't seem to understand as Candy pressed her head to her breast.

"It's okay, Cat, almost done," Jim said.

He pulled the probe out, but Cat was still upset, so he reached for her and pulled her onto his lap, wrapping his arms around her and holding her tight, rocking her. Maybe there was something comforting about him that Cat picked up on, as she pressed her head to his chest and started to calm down. She didn't push away, either. Candy was stunned, watching this man who seemed to be able to do so much more for Cat than anyone else could.

He looked over the little girl's tangled hair and said, "The reason she doesn't respond is because she's deaf."

Chapter 16

J im was still holding Cat in his lap, making a game out of examining her. He seemed to know what to do so she wouldn't freak out. "She's probably four or five," he said. "She's small for her age, and from what I can tell she's probably been deaf since birth. The natural brain development that happens for children is slowed when deafness isn't detected early. In developed countries, this is discovered when they're infants, more often than not. Slipping through the cracks still happens, though." He met Candy's gaze, and the knowledge that was there squeezed the muscles in her heart.

"Normal cognitive development, like learning and speech and language, doesn't happen in a child who's been left in a silent world where nothing can get to her brain. So much has been lost, and you can see in this child what I mean. Her development and learning has been stinted. The first thing people see is a learning disability or some handicap, but of course that isn't the case. Her brain has been deprived. She's still very much a baby. Do you understand what I'm saying?" he asked.

Candy was stunned. How could the orphanage have missed this? Couldn't deafness be spotted so easily? Then again, she'd missed it herself, blinded by Cat's overreactions to everything. "So are you saying there's no hope?" Candy said. "I can't believe that."

"No, I'm not saying that. There is sign language, of course, but with that you're still limited, and she'd still miss out on so much. The brain needs to develop, and without sound or a way for knowledge and learning to reach the brain, she can't even respond. You have to get the information to her brain, but first we have to figure out whether her hearing loss is treatable and then go with our options from there. Is it nerve related, an inherited condition, inner ear, or what?

"From there we can look into whether surgery is required, which can include repairing damage to the eardrum or bones in the inner ear. I can't tell from this cursory exam, and considering her circumstances, how much of a chance does Cat really have, considering the cost? If surgery is needed, she'll be just one of many children who'll never get it. Therapy is also required, but again, considering her circumstances, how much hope is there? She's missed so much," Jim said. He seemed so passionate, and he was now letting Cat play with the expensive probe. Pressing the button, Jim showed her in those few seconds how to flash the light.

"What if money wasn't an option? Where would we start with Cat?" Candy asked as she watched the girl sit calmly in Jim's lap. The doctor was filled with compassion and confidence, and he'd somehow reached Cat when no one else could.

"Well, first I'd want to examine her and do a complete workup. I presume we have no medical history, so we won't know if there was something unusual during the pregnancy or birth." Jim looked to Rafael and then Candy.

"As with all the children here, there'll be nothing. Many aren't even registered," Rafael said. He was leaning against the wall, his arms crossed. "You know how it is down here, Doctor Miller."

"That makes it difficult. Well, I'd like to complete a full exam. The tests I need to run are extensive, as there could be an underlying condition causing this. One of the hearing tests I'd like to run is a new one, an ASSR, which is done while she's sleeping. It would be best, considering we have a communication barrier. We'd need a specialist, as well," he said. He held his hand out to Cat, sliding the girl off his lap. Standing her in front of him as he opened his bag, he somehow managed to slip the doll back into her hand and take his probe. He stood up and looked down on the girl, who was watching him. "If you could bring her to my office so she can be fully assessed, I'll donate my time, but the tests will have to be paid for. They're expensive and require a hospital stay for the sedation. Can you make that happen?" he asked Candy. He then looked to the pastor, who nodded and also gestured to Candy.

"I can spare no one," Rafael said.

"I'll pay for whatever is needed," Candy said. "I'll bring her to you."

"Candy, let me ask you this. Are you prepared to become a guardian to this child, to make medical decisions for her? That's what this is going to take."

She swallowed because she realized what they were asking. If it had been just her, it would be an easy decision, but Neil was her husband, and she didn't know how she could convince him. Maybe she was wrong and not giving him enough credit. After all, he'd seen Cat's plight and had given the orphanage money. He wouldn't turn his back.

No matter what was dividing them now, she knew her husband had a heart. Of course he'd step in. She just needed to talk to him.

"Yes," she said, swallowing again.

"And your husband?" Rafael asked, and Jim gave her an odd look. She'd never told him she was married—but hadn't he noticed her ring? His expression became more closed.

"Of course he will," she said, though Rafael was watching her with an expression that said he thought otherwise.

Chapter 17

It was after dark when she pulled down the driveway in the dark green Explorer and parked behind the house next to Neil's Range Rover. Lights were on inside the house, but no one raced out to see her, not even her overprotective husband. She should have felt better for the breathing room, but she didn't, maybe because of how they'd parted earlier that day. With the issues between them with this surrogacy, she was starting to feel as if she was losing him.

She closed the door and listened to the night sounds. Instead of heading to the house, she went to the stable, where her horse and donkey were corralled. She slipped through the middle rail, and Sable called out to her. She wondered if her horse was asking where she'd been. Sable turned his head back to the bag of hay hooked inside the shelter and pulled out a mouthful. Meanwhile, Ambrose, the floppy-eared donkey she'd raised, was almost full grown. He wandered to her and rubbed his head against her stomach, and she hugged him and scratched his coarse fur. Then he, too, returned to his bag of hay, pulling out a few strands and munching away.

She loved spending time here with her animals. It gave her time to think and take in everything that had happened during the day. It was peaceful, which was something life hadn't been as of late.

"Candy?" Neil called from behind her.

She jumped, putting her hand on her chest. She hadn't heard him approach.

"Sorry, didn't mean to scare you." He kept walking to her but then turned toward a beam at the shelter a few feet away. He leaned against it, crossing his arms before looking down and taking in the ground, the animals, and then her. It was as if he needed time to get past all the hurt that had been festering between them for weeks now as well as their recent fight.

"Where have you been?" he asked. This time, he didn't sound angry or demanding or overbearing. His tone was more like resignation.

"At the orphanage," she said.

He nodded. "With that little girl?"

"Yes, with Cat." She watched Neil as he took in her animals, who were ignoring them and eating. "I found a doctor to see her," she explained. "She's deaf, Neil. She doesn't understand anyone, and that's the reason she acted so—so crazy and out of control."

Neil gave her all his attention. He didn't say anything, but he seemed to be absorbing what she was saying.

"There's help for her. She needs to be examined and tested. I said I would take her in to the doctor to see that she gets help," she said as Neil watched her. She didn't have a clue what he was thinking. He held everything back, and, right now, she wanted to reach out to him and share this with him, talk it out with him, hear his thoughts and ideas, but she was afraid of what he'd say.

"Candy, what are you thinking of doing? I gave Pastor Mendoza money to pay for her care, and my lawyer is making sure the authorities will leave her be. Why are you involved?"

That was the response she had been afraid of; cold and impersonal.

"Because she has no one, Neil," she said. "I want to be her guardian. Please, we could help her. We have so much to give, and she needs help. Whatever it is, we could do it!" She started toward him, her hand out to touch his arm, but she stopped when saw the look of horror on his face. Why couldn't he want this like her?

"Are you crazy?" he said. "Did you see her—what she did to you? What else is wrong with her? You don't know what kind of mess that child is, and you want to take her on? Candy, we have a baby on the way. You don't have time to care for some disabled child! Do you have any idea of the work you're talking about getting into? My God, look at Brad and Emily and the work involved with Trevor —and that's only with autism!" Neil could be nasty when he was upset about something, and this wasn't a side of him she'd seen until recently. When he was like this, she didn't want to be around him.

"I see," she said. "I never thought you saw your nephew as a burden. I don't believe your brother and his wife have ever acted as if Trevor's an inconvenience, either. I admire those two."

She watched his expression change. He looked away, shaking his head. "I didn't mean it like that, Candy. Trevor is Brad's biological son. He's my nephew. We look after our own. Of course he's not a burden, but why would you willingly take on a child who needs so much help but isn't even yours?"

"Emily did that, and she's not even Trevor's mother. Wasn't she the one who pulled the blinders off Brad's eyes and made him understand that his son had autism?" she said. She had him there, and she could tell she'd hit a nerve, too.

"Emily is a wonderful woman, Candy, and if it wasn't for her, I don't know where Brad and Trevor would be—but this isn't about them. This is about us. You should be here at home, getting ready for our baby, decorating a nursery, buying baby clothes or whatever you need to do to get ready."

"Decorating a nursery, are you kidding me?" She didn't know where to begin. How shallow did he think she was? "Neil, I really couldn't care less about buying paint and picking out colors for a room for a baby that doesn't even exist yet when there's a child, right in this town, who has nothing—not even a bed. She didn't ask for any of this to happen! She was tossed away like garbage. Maybe I wish I was more like Emily, having her courage."

He was shaking his head, his lips pressed together.

"I love you, Neil," Candy said, "but I'm sorry, I don't understand how we got here. I don't even know how to talk to you! Somehow I misunderstood your concern for Cat, when you tossed your money around. I guess you expected others to handle it for you. Like most wealthy people, you shoved all the dirty laundry away where it couldn't be seen and couldn't upset you. You can hire people to deal with the problem for you so you don't need to know about it, and then, as far as you're concerned, Cat won't exist." She couldn't hold back. She spewed all her hurt and disappointment right back at him. "Well, I'll be helping her. I'm not turning my back on her the way everyone else has. She needs me, Neil."

"I need you!" he shouted. He hit his chest with his fist, and the sound carried. "We have a baby coming who will need you!"

She wondered, as he took another step closer to her and pushed up his sleeves, whether he was planning on laying his hands on her. She took a breath before he could touch her. "We don't have a baby on the way yet," she snapped. "You just jerked off in a cup at a lab, and they fertilized some donor egg, and …"

Candy had to stop herself. She didn't know all the details, because Neil had never really shared them—just another aspect she was in the dark about. The only thing she remembered was what she had read in the contract. They were supposed to use a donor egg, but why would Maria have been at the clinic if Neil had just supplied a sample? It had to be stored, the egg harvested after it was fertilized. The insertion would come later, right? Neil's expression as he wiped his face with his hand gave her an awful sinking feeling.

"It wasn't a donor egg, was it?" she said, and Neil glanced away, ducking his head just enough to let her know he had done something he felt guilty about. Her world was bottoming out. "What did you do, Neil?"

"I'm sorry, Candy," he said. "I just wasn't convinced the donated egg that was being considered had been thoroughly screened for genetic problems. Maria already has been, which was one of the reasons Les sent her our way. Apparently there was another couple she was going to do surrogacy for months ago, and all her tests were done. She's ideal, and she wouldn't have agreed to a donated egg, anyway. She changed her mind." His expression was guarded, as if he was hiding something else from her, a piece of himself—as if he couldn't trust her with his secrets or his heart.

That was almost too much for her, and she felt a piece of her soul wither away. Her eyes burned, and she blinked furiously. There was no way she would shed a tear in front of her husband, the man she had married, who continued to pull the rug out from under her all because of his burning need for a child of his own. "I see," she said, swallowing the lump that sat like dry sawdust in her throat.

"What does it matter whose egg it is, hers or a donor's? She signed the contract," he said.

In that moment, she realized that Neil, a very smart man, had done something so very stupid, and he couldn't even hear the repercussions whispering in the shadows behind him. They would come back to haunt them, she knew, because nothing could be so easy. What was going through his head? He'd give up everything, including her, to have the baby he so blindly wanted.

"You're a fool, Neil," she said. There was no venom in her voice, only cold realization. "It matters, and we both know that, but you really don't care what I think, anyway. This is about you and what you want. Right now, I don't think there's a place for me in this journey you're on. You've made your decision, and I told you before I couldn't do this anymore. I didn't want a surrogate. This arrangement you've created … I'm not okay with any of this, and if you really took the time to sit back objectively, like you would in business, you would see just how stupid your decisions have been. You're a smart man, Neil, brilliant—except when it comes to your need to have a baby. In this, you're completely blind."

"Wow, Candy, that's just great. Now you're calling me stupid? Maybe you want to add that I'm a lying, cheating bastard, too."

She just stared at him, taking in the complete disconnect between them.

"You never told me you didn't want a surrogate, Candy. You said you wanted a baby, and you agreed, so don't you dare say that you were against this. You created quite the scene at my lawyer's office this morning, showing him how you don't trust me and you didn't believe that I had our best interests taken into consideration. You signed the agreement, so you don't get to go back and say you didn't agree to this!" He was in her face, his warm breath on her as he bit his words out. His expression was filled with so much animosity—it was as if a tide had turned in their relationship. The honeymoon was long gone.

"You're right, Neil. I signed that agreement—which specified that we would be using a donor egg. I may have had trouble deciphering the details of what I was reading, but I remember that part very clearly. I didn't agree to Maria being inseminated with your sperm and her egg. She's now the mother, and this is her child. I'm not a lawyer, but I can't help wondering how you can change the agreement without my signature. Are you trying to tell me the contract is still valid? I don't have a college degree, but I know it doesn't work that way."

He said nothing, his amber eyes closed to her. What was that saying? Lying eyes were hard to hide. "My lawyer did up a new contract," he said. "We didn't need your signature, as the change really only concerned Maria and myself."

His words hit her like a slap in the face. She had once thought she and Neil were invincible, with a love so strong it would see them through anything. She'd believed he had her back, but now she saw that it had been an illusion. Maybe he saw how much his words had hurt her, as he went to reach out to her. She pulled away.

"Candy, I didn't mean it that way," he said. "Of course you're a part of this. You're going to be a mother to this baby. It's just that it wasn't necessary for you to sign the contract this morning, as my lawyer pointed out. There really was no reason for you to be named on the contract, considering the change we made. It's just that all the legal jargon is so impersonal. I was trying to protect you and didn't want to upset you. I didn't want to bother you. At the end of the day, Candy, when we have our baby, you'll see how none of this mattered."

"Bother me?" she said. "Do you not understand that I have feelings—that I hurt and bleed? No, Neil, I didn't agree to this. I want a baby, yes, a child to raise and to love, but not the way you've gone about it. This whole thing with Maria is twisted, and you know what? The worst part is that I don't know everything. There should have been counseling!"

He sighed as if she was the problem, and she wanted to reach over and slug his arm.

"You only tell me what you want me to know," she said. "You keep everything else hidden from me. I didn't want a surrogate, and there's something about Maria and her mother that I don't trust. Maybe I didn't come right out and say, from the get-go, that I couldn't do this. I should have, and that's totally on me. I should have stood my ground, but I was feeling guilty for not being able to give you the one thing you wanted. I feel like I let you down." She couldn't stop the flood of emotions as her chin trembled.

Neil's expression softened, and he stepped closer, reaching out to touch her.

She moved away, shaking her head. "No, Neil. You can't make this better, not now."

"Look, we need to sit down and talk about this," he

said. "Let's go away, just you and me. We need time alone together. Our marriage is too important for us to not get past this. Don't you understand, I was just trying to protect you and make this happen for you? I made a vow to you! I married you, and I love you. I want to look after everything for you."

"Oh, Neil." She stepped right up to him and put her hands on his face. "I love you so much that it hurts, but you refuse to take any of my feelings into consideration. You won't listen to me, and you dismiss me as if my ideas and thoughts are irrelevant. You decide something and you just do it—to hell with how I feel. That's not a marriage. A marriage is you and me, you and me thinking together, deciding together, doing together. Why can't you get that? Maria and her mother … you've brought these people into our lives in a way that you knew I wouldn't be okay with." She stepped back, allowing her hands to fall to her sides. "By trying to protect me, you've opened the door to something that could have far greater implications than you can even imagine. I don't know what will happen, if anything, but I have a feeling that none of this will go as you expect it will."

"What are you, psychic?" he snapped, almost cutting her off. "Seriously, Candy, it sounds more like you don't trust me to take care of you, to protect you—to protect us," he said. He just wasn't hearing her, and she didn't know how to make him listen. They could go around in circles all night, becoming more resentful of each other.

"I'm taking Cat to the doctor tomorrow," she said. "I'm going to be her guardian."

Neil was looking at her, shaking his head. "You're doing exactly the same thing you just accused me of doing, so go and take a good long look in the mirror, my darling wife," he said. "You expect me to be okay with you giving everything of yourself to some girl who's going to need all your energy, all your attention? You haven't even discussed it with me, yet you expect me to be one hundred percent okay with this." He shook his head and started to walk away, gesturing with the flat of his hand. "No, you listen to me, honey. In Mexico, there are some laws you can't get around, and one of them is that a married woman can't file an orphan petition unless her husband joins. You're not a citizen of this country. You're an American, an outsider, just like me, but I have connections, and if I want to make something happen, I can."

The way he watched her with such hardness, she knew his stubbornness had kicked in. When Neil got like this, there was nothing anyone could do to change his mind, but what hurt more than anything was that she suspected he was right about the petition for guardianship. Would he really stand in the way of a little girl getting the help she needed because of some selfish, misguided notion he was harboring?

What did he really want from her? The only thing she was sure of was that he expected her to be available to him when he needed her, anytime, all the time—and that was something she was no longer going to be.

Chapter 18

"Where are you off to this morning so bright and early?" Rodney said as he walked around the front of his dark blue pickup to where Candy was holding the door to her SUV open. He was wearing worn blue jeans, a cowboy hat, and a western shirt. She always knew when he was heading out across the property to work with the ranch hands—and she also knew that the fact that he and Becky spent hours apart every day helped in the strong, loving relationship they had.

Rodney wasn't a man who told his wife what to do or how to think, though, and Candy was pretty sure he didn't pick out or buy her clothes for her. Why was Neil so controlling?

"I'm going into town," she said, "to the orphanage." She couldn't believe she'd said it, but she realized maybe she wanted his reaction, too.

He appeared confused but didn't look away. It was as if he was waiting for her to continue.

"There's a little girl there, very young, four or five. We've just learned she's deaf. No one knew, and she never got the help she needed. I'm going in to take her to the doctor and help her."

"Does Neil know?" Rodney asked. She wasn't sure whether that was approval she was hearing in his tone or whether he was of the same mind as Neil.

"I told him last night," she said, though she hadn't told him all the details about how she was planning on getting up first thing this morning to take Cat to see Jim Miller.

"That's a lot to take on, Candy. A child with any kind of special needs is a fulltime commitment."

"I know that, but what kind of person do you think it would make me to simply walk away from her when no one else will help her? I wouldn't be able to look myself in the mirror. Neil doesn't want me helping her, either."

"He may be concerned about you taking on too much. How will you find the time when you have a new baby to look after?" he said, sounding just like Neil.

"There's no baby yet," she said a little sharply.

Rodney cocked his head to the side, really taking her in. "We've noticed the tension between you and my son, of course. Neil can be rather strong willed. I guess all of us Friessen men are. We soften with age, though, realizing as time passes what's really important."

He was resting his arm and leaning on the hood of her SUV. She took in his dusty, worn cowboy boots and had to smile, as she couldn't imagine Neil wearing something that old and rustic.

"Did you ever try to arrange Becky, to tell her what to do and expect her to just do it, never stopping to include her?" she asked. She wondered by the odd look he gave her, was he thinking back on something he'd done or trying to figure out whether this was about her and Neil?

"My son is young, but he's smart as all hell, the only one of us to get his MBA," Rodney said. "Even at a young age, Neil was a natural in business. He was sharp, quick, two steps ahead of all of us. Just don't tell him that, or his head will swell even further." Rodney took a deep breath, looking away for a minute. There was no one around, just them under the bright morning sun. "Things were different in my day," he continued. "When I married Becky, it was really a time when a man was head of the household, more than now. Every decision he made had to be in the best interest of his family. Yes, I decided many things without telling Becky, and I never asked her, either. Did you know that when we got married, women would vow to obey their husbands?" He actually smiled and shook his head. "Becky never obeyed anything. She had a mind of her own from day one, and when she repeated that vow, I swear she sounded like she was spitting nails. You could see the trouble she had over that one."

"Times have changed, thankfully," Candy said, watching her father-in-law, who was taking her in with a wisdom that made her wonder whether he really knew the troubles between her and Neil. Maybe he did.

"That they have—but, Candy, a man's role is still to protect his family and look out for them. I taught my sons that, and that role will never change, no matter what vows are spoken. A man just isn't a man if he doesn't put his family first and know how to look after them. Neil married you, you're his wife. He may do things that he really believes are in your best interest, but we're human, Candy. We make mistakes. He better look after you."

"He brought a woman into our lives to carry his baby, and he's done something ..." She stopped because it felt like such a betrayal, talking this way behind his back.

"He hired a surrogate so he can have a child. I know what he's done, Candy. I can't imagine how you feel about it, but you have to work it out with your husband. Are you saying you don't want a child? I got the impression you do want children."

"I do want children, just not this way. It seems too personal, and I can't shake the feeling that some bigger problems have been set in motion."

"In what way?" Rodney asked. For a moment, she wondered whether she'd gone too far with what she was saying.

"This is hard for me, bringing in another woman, and I was excluded from the details. Did you know it's not a donor egg? Maria was inseminated. She refused the donor egg, and Neil didn't bother to tell me. That changes the entire game. She's now the mother, and what rights does she have?" Candy shook her head. "Supposedly, a new contract has been done up. I haven't seen it. We were supposed to have counseling, and …" She stopped talking. Even to her, this was starting to sound like a rant. "I'm sorry, I just don't like being in the dark this way. This isn't what I wanted, and I can't help feeling that any child that comes out of this will not be mine. It will be Neil and Maria's, and I'll be … I don't know where I'll fit in." She jingled her keys and looked down. Voicing her worst fears had made them feel so real.

"Hey, you listen to me," Rodney said. "I'm you're father-in-law, Candy, and we're family. What I'm going to say to you, you need to really listen to it. Neil, like all of us, is human, but he loves you, and whatever it is between you was worked out before you got married. Becky and I agonized over what you two went through when you lost the baby." He cleared his throat as if he was having a hard time finishing. "You almost died, Candy, and it tore my son up—all the blood …"

He stopped talking, and Candy watched. She'd never really considered everyone's feelings that blurry day so long ago when she'd collapsed before they were married. Their first wedding had been halted when she started bleeding at the altar. She remembered nothing but the pain, then waking up after surgery and being given that horrible news —she'd had an emergency hysterectomy from an ectopic pregnancy. Neil's family had been there, but Neil had had such a hard time coping that he'd distanced himself.

"Neil, as you know, didn't handle it well," Rodney said. "You scared the hell out of him. You were the first woman he ever really wanted, not just as a plaything but as a wife. You know Neil has this need to plan everything. He always has. Used to drive me and his mother a little crazy, at times. He's a realist, except when it comes to his family. Out of all my kids, Neil is the one who's most wanted children; a lot of children. You've seen him with his nieces and nephews."

She had seen him. It had been overwhelming and terrifying, because he had taken a responsibility and interest in those small children in a way she had never seen a man do before.

"He wants kids, always did," Rodney continued. "Becky and I wondered whether he'd actually walk away from you, because kids are a huge part of his plan, but you know what? Life sometimes doesn't work out as we plan. You need to make him listen to you, Candy. Neil would never do something to hurt you intentionally. There's one thing about my son, all my sons: we're about family, children, and our wives. Whether you and Neil adopt, don't have any children, or use a surrogate, it doesn't matter, Candy. It's about making your life together work. If he won't listen to you, you need to make him."

Rodney started to move away before tapping his hand on the hood of her SUV. "Running off to an orphanage to help out is admirable, Candy, but your first priority is your husband—and I'm not talking about sitting around and waiting for him. If you want to help this girl, you need to make your husband understand, or else you're doing exactly what you've just accused him of. That kind of rift festers between a couple. It becomes secrets and lies and goes places you don't ever want a marriage going." He touched the brim of his hat as he stepped back.

When Candy slid behind the wheel of the SUV and started the engine, she realized he was partly right, except what he didn't know was that the rift between her and Neil had already gone to those places.

Chapter 19

For two weeks, Candy had only glimpsed Neil here and there. They'd become two polite strangers sharing a bed, passing in the hall, and sharing the odd meal when he was home. Thankfully, Rodney and Becky had been away on a ten-day cruise of the Greek Islands, so at least she didn't have to see that questioning look in Rodney's eyes; the one he had given her two weeks ago before she left for the orphanage. Everything he said had made sense, but at the same time she wondered whether he was only seeing Neil's side of things.

He and Becky had to have picked up on the growing tension between her and Neil. There had been a time when she never would have believed she could sleep in the same bed as Neil without touching him. Over the past two weeks, he'd become extremely busy, staying away all day, most likely at the construction site, overseeing the building of his new resort.

When he did finally come home, she would usually be asleep or pretending to sleep, and in the mornings he was gone when she woke. The only way she knew he was there all night was that she could hear him breathing when she woke in the middle of the night from her restless sleep. She never touched him, although she was tempted. She wanted nothing more than to roll over and rest her head on his shoulder, feel his arm around her, pulling her against him and holding her in that way of his that made her feel she was safe, like nothing could ever hurt her again.

Her heart died a little more each night. She knew she couldn't avoid him anymore, and she had put off that much-needed talk for too long. The bedroom door was open, and she thought she heard him downstairs, talking to someone. She realized then, as she heard a car door and more voices, that it was Rodney and Becky home from their vacation. She paced the bedroom in her blue skirt and matching tank top, barefoot. She needed to speak with Neil—her Neil, the man with whom she had been through hell before they found their way back to one another. If they could find their way back to each other after the tragedies they had faced, why couldn't they now?

She was wringing her hands and then wiping at the dark circles under her eyes. She had to talk to him, to smooth things over, to come to some sort of an understanding, She couldn't live like this anymore. Rodney had been so right about all the secrets. She heard footsteps on the stairs, coming this way. Her heart hammered in her chest as she stared at the doorway, feeling all her courage slip away. She hurried around the corner to the bathroom and then stopped. *What is wrong with you, you coward?* She was acting like they were two strangers.

She started back to the bedroom, slipping around the corner, and Neil nearly bowled her over. He grabbed her arms, held her for a second, then slipped past her into the closet to choose a spotted red tie, sliding it under the collar of his white dress shirt without looking her way. She swallowed and realized she was nervous, being here with him. Her eyes burned, and her hands were shaking so hard that she gripped them. Should she leave? She shut her eyes for a second to get a grip. She had to talk to Neil—she didn't have a choice anymore.

How would he react after all the choices she'd made over the past week, all because of the rift they had created, a rift that had festered between them just like Rodney had predicted? The fact was that she hated needing Neil. She'd never wanted to need anyone again, but Neil had just had to have her. He had made her his, and she had loved it. She had been so foolish, giving him her heart. Right now, he was just holding on to it—not treasuring it as he'd promised. Sometimes, she wondered whether he was squeezing it just to hurt her.

When she looked up again, he was watching her.

"Neil, I need to talk to you," she said. Would he walk out the door or stay and listen to her? "I can't go on like this. I need to clear the air with you."

He finished doing up his tie, pushing the knot and setting his collar around it so neatly, so efficiently. She had once loved just watching him dress, but now there was no love in his expression. Was this how he was in business? It was a side of him she didn't want to know. He could be a hard man, but having all that hardness protecting her and being on her side had been different from having it all against her now.

"What do you want to talk about, Candy?" He sighed. "Maria is pregnant. She just found out. It's early, but it's real."

She didn't know what to say. She'd been so wrapped up

in her own world, with Cat, taking her to Jim and letting Rafael believe she and Neil were applying for guardianship. She'd paid for the tests with Neil's money without once asking him. He had to know by the amount she was spending, but he never said anything. This was all too much.

"I didn't know," she said. "I guess congratulations are in order."

She couldn't make herself sound happy. Now what? She couldn't make the baby go away. This baby was Neil's, everything he'd ever wanted—except he was having it with another woman. It felt like cheating, even though that didn't make any sense. She couldn't say anything to anyone, as they wouldn't understand.

"I wish it could have been you," he said. He was watching her softly and wistfully, even with this distance between them. His gaze burned into her, and she blinked back tears. That kind of miracle just wasn't possible.

"Me too," she whispered. He was blurring in front of her, so she looked away, taking a breath to steady herself and putting her hands over her empty abdomen, where her womb had once been.

She felt him step closer. His hands were around her, pulling her against him so that she could rest her head against his chest. She had missed this so much, just being in his arms. Neil had a lot of faults, but when he held her, when he gave her all of his attention, when he made love to her ... she could believe that she was all that existed for him in those moments. Being in his arms could almost make everything bad that had come between them disappear for a while.

"I love you," she whispered.

"I know you do," he said as he rested his chin on top of

her head. It was such an easy fit, and it was so automatic, how her arms slid around his waist and held him. She breathed him in. There was such strength in his scent that she wanted to let him take care of everything just like before. It would be so easy.

His hands slid up to her face, her cheeks, holding her. He pressed a kiss to her forehead and her lips before moving back. He didn't let her go, and she slid her hands over his and looked up at him. The hardness in his eyes had softened. "We do need to talk about a lot of things," he said, "including Cat. You've been taking her to these appointments and checking her into the hospital for tests, and the amount of money you spent on these medical procedures … you never said one word to me, Candy."

"I'm sorry, Neil. I should have asked you before spending your money."

"Candy, stop. It's not about the money. I would have spent it gladly. You should have talked to me, though. Did you know I got a phone call from the hospital about our application for orphan petition, which you signed for me. They said you told them an original copy would follow, notarized by our lawyer. They're waiting, Candy. You lied to them."

She shut her eyes. She had panicked when taking Cat to the hospital for the hearing test where she had to be sedated. If the hospital hadn't had the paperwork, Cat wouldn't have been admitted. Candy was horrified now at how she'd taken that paper and scribbled her husband's name. He was right. What she had done was wrong. She was digging herself in so deeply, with so many lies, just to help this child.

"I'm sorry, Neil. I didn't know what to do. I didn't realize what a mess it was, and I didn't think at the time.

She's not registered. We don't even know who her parents are, where she was born … When the appointment was scheduled, they would have turned her away. I couldn't have that. I panicked. I—"

"Stop it!" he said. "Candy, you're trying to help this little girl in a country that isn't really helpful to outsiders. You're not even a citizen of Mexico. We're Americans, Candy, and you can get us into a lot of trouble. Does Pastor Mendoza know what you've done?" Neil stepped away from her, and Candy sank down on the bed, her legs feeling like limp noodles. She just shook her head.

"He'd never have let me take her. She has no one, Neil. She needs someone to speak for her, to help her."

"Why does it have to be you?" he shouted, his hands in the air. Then he stepped back, shutting his eyes for a second before putting his finger and thumb over the bridge of his nose, his way of trying to calm down when he'd gotten himself worked up. She'd only seen him do this a time or two, but it gave her an idea of how mad he was. He sighed. "Why, Candy? Why do you feel it has to be you? I gave Rafael Mendoza a lot of money to hire someone for the girl. Let him hire someone who knows what they're doing. I'll bring someone in to help her if that's what you want, but you need to walk away."

It hurt so much that she couldn't get him to understand. "I can't explain it, Neil. When she looked up at me that first time, there was something there that I couldn't turn my back on. I need to do this for her. No one else is going to fight for her like I can. There's help she can get. Jim told me about a cochlear implant for deaf children that will provide a sense of sound. It's an expensive surgery, and it can't be done here—" She stopped. He was staring at her with the same hardness as earlier. What had she said to make him revert back to this?

"Jim?" he asked. There was a tick in his cheek from how tightly he was holding himself.

"Jim Miller," she said. "He's the doctor I've been taking Cat to. He's very good. In fact, I got his name from the nurse at the fertility clinic that day a few weeks ago."

Neil was just shaking his head again.

"I don't want to fight with you, Neil. I'm trying to share this with you, but I don't know how anymore. I don't know where I fit into your life!" she cried out, standing up. She was shaking again as she watched him pace.

"You're jealous of Maria, but here you are, spending time with a doctor you're on a first-name basis with. How familiar is this man with you, Candy?"

The way he said it, she knew he was thinking the worst. How could he? She wasn't like that. Why would he even go there? "Neil, I would never cheat on you. I would never let another man put his hands on me. He's been helping Cat," she said. Was her nose growing, though? They had shared a coffee or two, and it had been friendly, both of them chatting about their pasts. They were becoming friends through helping the little girl, but Candy knew her husband would never understand. Neil would never be okay with her being friends with another man. He was still watching her. "Are you going to walk out that door on me?" she asked.

How could they resolve anything now? She wondered whether Neil had had enough. She'd lied about the papers, and even though Neil had gone ahead with the surrogate, making decisions without her and even changing the contract behind her back, two wrongs didn't make a right. She hated this feeling of needing Neil, being at his mercy. For the first time, she understood how women must have felt a hundred years earlier, when they had no rights at all. This powerlessness … how had she found herself in this position? If Neil chose to walk away and leave her, she didn't know what she'd do.

"What kind of man do you think I am, Candy? Do you think I would toss you to the wolves? After what you've done …" He stopped and shut his eyes again for a second. She knew he was doing his best not to lose it. He pumped his fists as if trying to work off his anger. They had both been saying such harsh and unkind things lately. Did he regret marrying her?

"I'm sorry, Neil. That's all I can say. I wish I could go back and change what I did. I would have called you. I would have …" It was wishful thinking, really.

He was shaking his head. "Candy, you can't go back. You're not being realistic. This is what happens when you get caught doing something you shouldn't."

For a minute, she watched him, wondering who he was. Neil had never been like this with her before, so unforgiving. "We've drifted so far from each other," she said. "I don't know how to reach you. When we talk, we fight. I should have said something, and I'm sorry, but that little girl didn't ask for this to happen to her. They had to sedate her for the test, and I knew they'd turn us away if I didn't have the papers. I couldn't do that, so I lied. I would probably do it again. If that makes me a bad person in your eyes … well, I'm sorry."

"Candy, what you did was admirable, trying to help, but you lied to me! You committed fraud by signing my name. You could go to jail for something like that."

"Are you trying to scare me? I know I shouldn't have done it. I didn't even think of the consequences. What are you going to do?" she asked. Her voice squeaked. She was terrified.

"I'm going to get you out of it, but don't you ever do

something like this again. I need to be able to trust you," he said.

He watched her for a moment. Instead of feeling as if she and Neil had cleared the air, Candy felt as if this had become one more thick wall between them. Would they ever be able to get past this?

<h1 style="text-align:center">Chapter 20</h1>

"I cannot believe you would do something like this!" Pastor Mendoza cried, running his hands through his rumpled dark hair. His worn plaid shirt was rolled up to the elbows, his blue jeans faded and torn at the knee. He looked like a bum today, and she could almost hear Neil judging him in her head even though he hadn't said a word.

Neil was leaning against the wall in Pastor Mendoza's office, still in his white dress shirt, red tie, and black dress pants. Not a hair was out of place, and his arms were crossed. Both men stared at Candy as she stood alone in the middle of the small office.

"I was trying to do what was right for Cat, trying to help her. How could that be wrong?" She didn't know what else to say to make this better. Maybe she was being foolish to believe this wasn't as bad as it seemed.

"You will sign the petition, Mister Friessen, to save your wife?" Rafael asked.

Neil didn't say anything. Candy knew he didn't want to

be involved, and not once during the drive here had he said he would sign the petition.

"I'll send it over to my lawyer to handle," he finally said. He hadn't really answered the question, and Candy was starting to sweat.

Maybe the pastor noticed this, as he said, "You're very lucky your husband will protect you. In Mexico, the laws are not so friendly. You're considered guilty first and must prove your innocence. I'm afraid, Mister Friessen, that your wife signed your name for you. I have a copy, and she gave the document to the hospital. There will be questions as to why they haven't received it. They've called twice. Candy, you said two days ago that the lawyer had it and you would call and follow up. You have to tell Doctor Miller what you've done."

No, she couldn't do that. She'd looked him in the eye and lied to him, too. She didn't think she could stand if he knew the truth. She said nothing and stood there with her hands clasped together.

"I've hired a private detective to find Cat's parents," Neil said, staring at the pastor. He was ignoring Candy, as if she wasn't even there. He was looking for her parents, but what it felt like was that he was trying to take Cat away from Candy any way that he could. She could feel her heart breaking a little more.

"That's very good, but I wouldn't hold out much hope, Mister Friessen."

"We'll see. One way or the other, I don't want my wife involved anymore. I want you to hire someone to look after the girl and get her the help she needs. I specifically left you money for that before. This time, please look after it. We have a baby on the way."

The pastor gave her an odd look. She knew he was about to congratulate her.

"It's not me," she said. "I'm not pregnant. I can't have children. It's the one thing I can't give my husband. He's found another woman to give him one." It sounded so crude.

"Stop it, Candy," Neil said. "It's a surrogate. Candy had to have a hysterectomy, an emergency. She almost died."

She turned. Neil had never said it that way before. For a moment, he sounded sad.

The pastor was shaking his head. The sympathy on his young face was almost too much. "So your husband has arranged for a surrogate, and you're unhappy about this, Candy?"

She wanted to cry. No one really understood. "This is about Cat," she said. "Doctor Miller has done many tests, and he's talked about a procedure for a cochlear implant that would give her her hearing back—"

There was a knock on the open door, and Jim Miller stepped in. Candy didn't have to see Neil's face to know that he was glaring at the light-haired, handsome man, whose gaze went right to her.

"Candy, that's not quite right," Jim cut in. "The quality of sound she'll get is different from natural hearing, with less sound information processed by the brain. The procedure can only be done if she has a functioning auditory nerve. This surgery is expensive, Candy, and it's a long, grueling process. She'll have to learn sound, words … like a baby. She'll be terrified, and with the therapy she'll need, years and years of it, she may never recover all the lost time. And there's something else—the procedure can't be done here."

Why did it feel as if Jim was now on her husband and Pastor Mendoza's side? The way Neil was watching her, she could see that he was taking in everything that was being said. Candy wondered whether it could get any worse. The fact was that, right now, she really didn't care how much trouble she was in. The news Jim was offering wasn't good.

"I thought you could do the surgery," she said. Her hands were shaking, and she jammed them in her long, knotted hair and swept it back. She must have looked a sight. Maybe that was why Neil was looking at her the way he did. He wasn't happy with her, and she was the opposite of his tidiness.

"No, Candy, I can't do the surgery. I'm sorry if I ever gave you that impression. In a best-case scenario, with a functioning auditory nerve, the cochlear implant would probably work, but Mexico doesn't have what she needs. I'm sorry, Candy. You would need to leave Mexico and go to the United States. I have a friend in Phoenix, Arizona, a neurologist, who can do the surgery—"

"It can't happen," Pastor Mendoza said, interrupting him and gesturing to Candy. "The best thing to do is teach her sign language. Many get by with just that, and it's fine. She'll be able to communicate then. This all sounds eccentric and unnecessary."

"She'll be limited in what she can do," Jim said. "Signing is fine to start, and I agree she should learn, but I'm of the school of thought that you're looking to enrich her life, not limit her communication. I would recommend the implant. It would provide her opportunities that others in the deaf community—"

"The surgery is not possible," Rafael interrupted. "Candy, would you like to tell Doctor Miller why?"

Candy shut her eyes as the attention all focused on her. When she glanced over at Jim, she wanted to beg his forgiveness. She prayed he wouldn't hate her. "I'm so sorry," she said. "I did something I shouldn't have. I forged my husband's signature on the orphan petition for Cat."

She met his gaze, but what she saw in his eyes wasn't condemnation and anger, as she'd seen in Rafael's and Neil's—it was understanding.

Chapter 21

"So you're not under house arrest," Jim said.

For the first time in days, Candy couldn't hide the smile that touched the corner of her mouth as she walked beside him down the busy tourist-filled street in Cancun. Jim Miller had a wicked sense of humor, and when she glanced his way, she didn't miss his mischievous smile. He had a smile that lit up his entire face. He was the absolute opposite of her husband in almost everything. He was disorganized and always running behind, forgetful at times, and sloppy. He did still hold the doors open for her, though, and he teased her often, seeming to get a kick out of making her blush.

"No, I'm not," she said. "I'm sorry again for what I did, Jim, and for lying to you."

He kept walking beside her, and they stopped by a street-side vendor making deep-fried bananas. He handed the woman some money and took the fast food packet. "I'm absolutely addicted to these things," he said, holding out the carton. "Here, take one."

She started to say no. Neil would never stop at a street

vendor and pick up something like this. Maybe that was why she reached over and picked out a piece, slipping it into her mouth and chewing.

"See? Totally bad for you. You've got to live a little."

She actually giggled, and she put her hand to her mouth as she chewed and then swallowed.

"You should smile more, Candy," he said. "You're very beautiful."

She looked away, uneasy with the compliment.

"I wasn't hitting on you, so don't get all weird on me," he said with a laugh. "If I was hitting on you, you'd know it. Anyway, I admire your courage for what you did."

She kept walking with him down the busy sidewalk, and they took the stairs down to the sandy beach. "It was stupid," she said. "Neil is still barely speaking to me. He's talked to the hospital himself, but I don't know what was said. Maybe he decided to tell them what I did. Maybe he's done with me." She sounded pitiful to her own ears.

"No, he didn't. The hospital stopped calling the clinic. Your husband bailed you out. His lawyer sent over a notarized copy with his signature."

She didn't realize she'd been holding her breath until she breathed easier.

"I guess he wanted you to suffer a bit," Jim said, "not tell you so you could sweat and worry, wondering if the Mexican police would show up on your doorstep. That wasn't very nice on his part, but I'd probably have done the same."

"Hey!" Candy shoved his shoulder and stumbled a bit. "You jerk."

The sound of his laughter made her feel so much lighter than she had felt in a long time.

"So what are your plans for Cat?" he asked, offering

her another fried banana. He was right; they were addicting.

"Rafael used my husband's money to hire someone to teach her sign language, but I want to find a way to get her to your friend in Arizona." She looked shyly over at him, half expecting to see that she'd gone too far. Maybe he'd say enough was enough and just walk away, but he had a grin on his face, and she suspected there was a light in his brilliant blue eyes, hidden behind his dark glasses.

"Can you get your husband to go along with it, rush the petition? They normally take years here, and then you have US immigration to deal with—a lot of red tape," he said, but he was making it sound as if there was another way.

"I'll try, but Neil's not talking to me. His focus is elsewhere right now." She stopped herself from saying Maria's name. Neil wasn't talking to her, but he was talking to Maria every day. Every time his cell phone rang, it was her. She called him, he called her—like two overjoyed lovers.

"Earth to Candy." He nudged her gently. "You're saying your husband is focused on the surrogate carrying his child."

She looked up. "Yeah."

"It sucks, Candy. That's all I can say."

"It was supposed to be a donor egg, but then something happened and she changed her mind. Neil never told me."

He was giving all of his attention to her, watching her, listening.

"It hurt that he never told me. He just went along with it, said he had her sign another agreement and I didn't need to be involved."

"Wow, that's harsh. It sounds as if you don't believe him," he said, voicing her worst fear.

"Right from the beginning, when he mentioned surrogacy, I had this awful feeling, but he just went ahead and arranged it. He met with this young woman, Maria, and her mother. I didn't want it to happen, and I should have tried harder to tell him how I felt. Now she's pregnant with his child—their child."

"And it hurts," he said, finishing her thought for her.

"It hurts," she said. "I don't know what to do anymore except ride it out, count the days, and pray for … I don't know, peace?"

"I don't mean to throw salt on your wound, but I've seen and heard enough of these cases to know they rarely go smoothly. You've already had some red flags waving." He stopped as if not wanting to say any more.

"And … ? Come on, Jim," she said. "Please don't hold back."

He finished chewing and then stopped at a garbage can to toss the empty package away, wiping his hands together and brushing the crumbs from his mouth. "There are a lot of things to think about when you're considering a surrogate. They need to be emotionally grounded, and of course there has to be a clean past, with no family history of genetic problems, illnesses. You really want a full background check done when you have a genetic connection, as you do now, since Maria is the mother." He watched her closely, crossing his arms. She could tell he cared. "Your husband's name will go on the birth certificate, and there'll be a stepparent adoption for you," he continued. "The problem is that in Mexico, in this state, that's not legal. The baby legally will belong to the birth mother. If you had gone to Guadalajara, this would be a different story."

She was frozen. Neil was not a stupid man. He didn't make mistakes like this.

"I'm not saying Mexico outlaws surrogacy," Jim said,

"but they have no laws for when this baby is born. Therein lies your problem. California, which has the best laws for you, states that whoever is named the legal parent in the contract prior to conception has all legal rights when the child is born. In the best-case scenario, you find a way to get her to California and out of Mexico."

"So what you're saying is that Neil and I may never be rid of this woman."

Jim slid off his glasses and really looked at her. "No, she may always be a part of your husband's life." He shook his head. "I would never do that to you," he murmured, and as she watched him, she had a feeling that, this time, his interest was more than just that of a friend.

Chapter 22

When Candy arrived home, she noticed a small brown car parked in front of the house. Instead of pulling down the driveway and around back, she parked behind it and went in the front door. She heard voices coming from the living room and noticed, as she walked in, that Neil was sitting in a chair, talking with someone. As she went closer, she realized it was Maria. She was in an easy chair with her feet up, her face glowing as she listened to Neil. Candy went down the three steps, and everyone's eyes went to her.

"Hi," she said to Neil, wondering what she should do as she took in Carmen sitting on the sofa, looking up at her.

"Are you sure your wife will be okay with this arrangement?" Carmen asked.

Candy glanced over at Neil as he ran his finger over the indent under his lower lip. He flicked his gaze awkwardly up to her and then took a breath, putting his hand down on the arm of the chair. "Candy will be fine with this, Carmen."

"Fine with what, Neil?" She glanced over at the mother and daughter, who shared an odd look. She really hated being the odd man out, and she was really beginning to hate all these secrets between her and Neil.

"Maria had some cramping, spotting," Neil said.

Candy found herself holding her breath, hoping Maria had lost the baby. Immediately, she felt ashamed for having that thought. "Oh" was all she could choke out.

"The baby's fine, Missus Friessen. Nothing to worry about. My Maria is strong, but the doctor wants her off her feet, on bed rest," Carmen added.

As Candy looked back at her husband and the dark look he leveled at Carmen, she realized there was more going on and she wasn't going to like it.

"Maria is going to be staying with us," Neil said, "until the doctor says it's safe—"

Candy didn't wait for Neil to finish. She gave him her back and didn't miss the startled expressions and gasps from Carmen and Maria as she walked out of the living room. At this point, she didn't care.

"Candy!" Neil called after her, but she didn't stop as she climbed the stairs at a jog to their room. She just slammed the door and lay on the bed as the door flew open.

"What the hell was that, Candy? I've never known you to be rude," Neil snapped. The door closed behind him.

All she did was turn her head and look at him, her cheek pressing into the soft duvet, her hands folded under her face. "You bring another woman into our house and you don't even have the decency to talk to me first—to see if I might have a problem with it?"

Neil didn't move from the door. "Candy, I'm getting tired of this with you. Where were you, anyway? When Maria called from the doctor, I looked everywhere for you and then found your SUV gone. You've taken to sneaking off now?"

He was making her sound like a child. She just lay there and watched him, trying to figure out how their relationship had turned into this. Had he always been this domineering? No, not like this. It seemed as if he was expecting her to ask permission to leave the house.

"What exactly is our relationship, Neil?" she asked. She watched the confusion in his expression.

"What kind of games are you playing, Candy?"

"I'm not, but you seem to be. You expect me to report to you like a child, ask your permission to go out?" She moved to sit on the bed, kicking off her shoes and crossing her legs.

"Of course you're not a child, Candy. It's not about asking permission. It's about being respectful so I'm not worrying and wondering that something happened to you. As of late, you've just taken off without saying anything. If I call your cell phone, you don't answer."

"Why are there two sets of standards here? You do whatever you want without discussing it with me, but I'm expected to report every detail to you."

"Whoa." He appeared taken aback by her response, and she could sense they were approaching the point of no return, where things could be said that might never be taken back. "Candy, I never just leave without telling you I'm going. Have you ever gone looking for me in the house to find that I've just taken off?"

She found herself trying to think back to find a time, but her cheeks began to heat, because she knew he'd never left without saying a word. She may not always have known where he was going or with whom he was meeting, but in all fairness, when he went out, he always let her know.

"I can tell from your lack of response that you know I'm right," he said.

She covered her eyes with the palm of her hand and rubbed, then glanced up at him where he stood at the foot of the bed, arms crossed, watching her. "You're right. I'm sorry. I'll let you know if I'm going out."

He just stared at her, trying to figure her out.

"Neil, I'm not living in the same house with the woman carrying your baby. Why would you bring her here, and why would you do that to me and not believe I would be upset? You know how much this has come between us now." She shook her head, feeling such misery. They were fast coming to that point she didn't want to face—a life without Neil. Right now, it seemed as if he'd already stepped out of their marriage.

"You need to be stronger than this, Candy." He sat on the edge of the bed and leaned on his hand beside her. "We're in this with Maria together. How many times do I need to tell you to stop worrying? Everything is going to be fine. I'm starting to get the feeling that you're creating problems that aren't even there. When are you finally going to believe me that everything will work out?"

"Neil, it's not fine. Nothing is fine with us. We don't even talk anymore, we fight. You never touch me. When was the last time we made love? I don't want this between us, and I don't want Maria here. It's just too much to ask of me."

"Candy, I need you to trust me about Maria. She'll be in bed, resting. Ana will be looking after her, and I'll bring in a nurse. She'll be no problem, and this is only until she makes it to sixteen weeks. Until then, it's too dangerous for her to be alone. She needs to be waited on, and I can arrange that for her."

"Does it matter what I think, Neil, really? If I continue

to say no, will you listen to me?" She needed to know where she stood with him. "You already pay for an apartment," she said, although they'd never even discussed that. Knowing anything about Maria just hurt too much.

"I put them in a house."

"Who?" she asked.

"Carmen and Maria, I bought them a house. Carmen works during the day, though, so she can't look after Maria," Neil said, as if there was no other solution.

"Neil, why not just pay Carmen to stay home and look after her daughter? Why didn't you mention any of this to me?"

"Stop it, Candy," he said. She could tell he was holding something back.

"You did offer, right? You could hire a nurse to take care of her."

Neil just shook his head. "Look, with something like this … I talked to the doctor, and I need to make sure she doesn't get up, that she stays in bed, eats well—"

"You want to watch your baby grow inside her," Candy said. This time, Neil had the good grace to blush. "Why didn't I see this coming?"

"Candy, look, we're in it this far. Just don't make a problem out of something that isn't."

"Are you sure there isn't a problem, Neil? From where I'm sitting, there are red flags waving everywhere. Now you're moving Maria in, and Maria is the mother of your child, so yes, their could be problems. Your name goes on the birth certificate, and so does hers. Me? I'm the outsider and have to adopt, so this really is your child and hers, not mine. In Mexico, there are apparently no laws around surrogacy, so how're you going to ensure everything is fine? Do you really think she isn't going to bond with this baby she's carrying—which is hers? Legally, you can't take this baby away from her, and you've now moved her under our roof."

"Candy, she signed a contract. She agreed. I've paid her money There's one thing in Mexico—they may not have laws in this state around surrogacy, but everything comes down to money and who you know. Tell me, Candy, who's filling your head with all these problems?"

She knew she shouldn't say anything, but when she opened her mouth, his name slipped out: "Jim Miller."

Chapter 23

It had been seven days since Maria moved into the estate. She had been set up in a bedroom across the hall from Neil and Candy's master suite, and Candy wondered whether Neil had deliberately stuck her in there so that every time she left their bedroom, she had to pass Maria's open door and see her propped up in bed, listen to her soft voice on the phone, or pass Ana in the hall, carrying a tray to her room. It was hard. It was hurtful.

She felt a part of herself, the good part, slowly dying every day.

Neil had lost his temper and slammed his fist in the wall above her head when she told him about Jim and what he had told her about problems with the surrogacy. She had leapt off the bed, half angry and half terrified. Evidently, it was okay for him to talk to Maria but not for her to talk to Jim. She got that loud and clear. He had double standards and a jealous streak that she hadn't realized ran so deep.

She now spent her days sneaking around—avoiding Neil, avoiding Maria, avoiding everyone. Neil was no longer interested in spending much time with her, and she was starting to feel she was more of a nuisance to have around, even though he had told her not to worry. For seven days, she and Neil hadn't had a conversation as husband and wife. He got up, showered, dressed, and checked on Maria. She got up, showered, dressed, and left, spending every free moment at the orphanage with Cat.

She'd learned sign language. The first time the little girl signed the word for *thirsty,* Candy had cried. Every time that Cat saw Candy, she flew into her arms and hugged her. Right now, Cat was the only one who needed her. She doubted very much that, if she left now, Neil would even notice, and she felt such sadness at that thought.

When she opened the bedroom door and stepped out into the hallway, her heart thudded when she realized Neil was there. He had his back to her as he walked into Maria's bedroom, talking to her the same way he had once talked to Candy. She knew she should leave, walk away and not watch, but when he sat beside her on the bed and Maria just gazed at him the same way that Candy once had, she felt her heart bleed. Maria was in love with him, of course. What woman wouldn't be? By the way Neil sat beside her on the bed, leaning on his other hand over her legs, she could see the closeness growing between them. Their connection was unbreakable. A baby—who could top that? No, she'd be a fool not to face the reality of the situation. Neil wanted a baby, a family, and Candy couldn't give that to him. Maria was carrying his baby, and he would watch every day as her belly swelled. He would touch her belly, feel his child kick, and recognize the bond growing between them. Candy would always be on the outside, looking in.

She lowered her head and started down the stairs, keeping her footsteps as quiet as possible. She didn't miss

Rodney lingering at the bottom of the stairs, staring up at her as she came down. She stopped at the bottom, swallowing the lump, willing herself not to cry as her eyes burned. She looked up at her father-in-law, so tall, with his short, gray hair neat and tidy. He knew, and he watched her and put his hand on Candy's arm. She lowered her head and wept, choking back her sobs so she wouldn't make a sound. Her shoulders shook, and Rodney pulled her into his arms and just held her, guiding her into the living room and sitting her on the sofa. He sat on the coffee table in front of her, clasping his hands in front of him as she wiped the tears from her cheeks with the back of her hand.

He glanced over at the stairs and then back at her. "Becky and I have stayed out of your business, but I'm wondering if it's past time I don't step in and have a talk with my son."

Candy reached out and touched his arm. "Rodney, I can't take much more of this. I'm only human, with real feelings. To see my husband move another woman into our home and—" She choked. It was impossible, talking about this nightmare she was living, having the only man she'd ever loved turn his back on her for a baby another woman was carrying. It hadn't started that way with Maria, but that was the reality of where they were right now.

"What am I going to do?" she asked Rodney, already knowing the answer, though it broke her heart to even consider it.

"Let me talk to him. This has gone too far with Maria. Maybe you and Neil should go away together. You need time to work this out."

She found herself reaching out and touching Rodney's hand. "Do you remember how you warned me about this rift between me and Neil, and the festering? Well, I'm afraid it may be too late. I don't know what to do, but I won't sit here in this house any longer while he shoves this woman in my face."

"You need to stop and think about this," Rodney said. "Marriage is a lot of work, and Becky and I … well, it hasn't always been easy. I did some things I'm not proud of. She'd have had every right to divorce me, but she didn't. She forgave me."

Candy wondered what Rodney had done that was so bad. He didn't seem too willing to share, though, so Candy didn't want to push. When she heard Neil coming down the stairs, she wiped her eyes again and stood up, moving out of the way, taking on a happy expression that faded when his gaze landed on her. She couldn't smile at him. She stared at him like a stranger. She could feel Rodney watching both of them.

"Neil, it's time you and I have a talk," Rodney said. He started to his son as he stood up to his full height.

Neil just shook his head. "Dad, it's going to have to wait. Maria has a doctor's appointment, and I need to take her in."

That was all Candy heard as she stood across from Neil, feeling as if they were on opposite sides of a conti-nent and neither was willing to give in to the other. "Have a great day" was all she could say as she hurried away to the front door, grabbing her keys and clutching her cloth purse. She pulled open the door and jogged down the steps, freezing when she realized she had parked around back. She'd just been looking for an escape.

The door opened behind her. "Candy," Neil called to her. Her heart jumped. There were birds—crows, maybe —cawing in the background, fighting over something.

"Yes?" She turned to face him, a stranger in the body

of the man she loved. He started down the stairs toward her.

"Where are you going today?" he asked. He stopped an arm's length from her.

"To see Cat," she said.

He looked away and nodded. "Just to let you know, I heard from the guy I hired to locate her family. He's found a grandmother. He's trying to locate the mother, but she works at the market and has two other kids."

For a moment, she was too stunned to say anything. She couldn't even begin to absorb what he was saying. She just nodded as waves of anger rolled through her. How could people just abandon their child? She couldn't imagine an excuse, because as far as she was concerned, there wasn't one. "And they want her back?" She held her breath as she asked, worried about what he'd say.

Neil didn't say a word. Maybe he was just waiting for another way to hurt her. "I don't know yet. I still need to talk to them. I was planning on going to see the grandmother."

She watched him, waiting for what was next. Did he expect her to want to go? For the first time, she didn't want to share anything with Neil for fear of what he'd do. "I see. So your objective is to take everything from me. You're not happy that I found someone who actually needs me, this child, because it's taking me away from what exactly, Neil? Do you want me to wait here, having my heart ripped out over and over, watching you with another woman, caring for her, talking to her as you once did me? Do you somehow think I'm okay with this, coming out of our bedroom and seeing her across the hall—and you always in there with her? She's in love with you!" She turned away, squeezing her purse strap, not having a clue what to do next but to get away from him and the ache that over-whelmed her when he was near.

"You're just going to walk away?" he snapped. He reached out and grabbed her arm, and she went to fight him and pull away, but he wouldn't let go. There was hurt and anger and something else in his eyes, an expression she couldn't believe was even there.

"What do you expect me to do, Neil? You've hurt me so badly with your indifference, yet you somehow believe I'm just going to stay here and watch you——"

"I expect you to be my wife!" he shouted. "To share this baby, this experience, with me. This is for us, Candy. I don't know what's going on with you. You said you wanted a family, children, and this is the only way it can happen." He was yelling, and everyone could hear him, but it was the way he said it that bothered her. Was he blaming her?

"When I married you, Neil, we had so much to work through, so much we had to get past. I knew you blamed me after the hysterectomy."

"Oh, for God's sake, Candy, we're past that! You know what? Maybe I did, at the time, because you should have said something. I was hurt that you hid how you had been cramping, and you said nothing to me, and you let it get so bad you collapsed, and by a sheer miracle they were able to save you when your tube ruptured. If you'd have said something, I would have taken you to the doctor, you would have gotten help, they would have found the problem—and, right now, you'd be the one pregnant. I'd be waiting on you, loving you and watching our child grow inside you." He was almost spitting, he was so angry.

She glanced away. He was right. She had blamed herself, too, but having him throw it back in her face now was cruel. His hand slid away, dropped to his side. He wiped his face, and she could tell he was ashamed of what he'd said.

"I'm sorry. I shouldn't have said that."

"Why? It's the truth. I wondered, Neil, how you really felt."

He tried to reach out to her, and she had to step back. The hurt was too raw between them. "Look, Candy, come inside and let's talk about this. I think we've both gotten to a point where we've said things we shouldn't. I don't understand why you can't trust me to know what's best."

She just stared at him, and her heart broke a little more. "I think maybe it's best if I leave," she finally said.

Chapter 24

It was unusual today how the clouds had moved in, turning a bright summer day in this part of Mexico uneasy. The weather matched her life right now. Sitting in Jim's waiting room with children and parents all around her, chattering away, she couldn't even hear the commotion around her.

"Hey, are you okay? I was calling you," Jim said. He was right in front of her, touching her hand, leaning down. It felt so surreal, and she took in his worry, the tiny lines around his eyes. He was wearing a light blue t-shirt today, with blue jeans. His light hair, she noticed, had a natural wave to it that was a little unruly. "Whoa, you're not okay. Come on." He had her arm and led her down a hall and into his office. He sat her in a chair and shut the door, and then he was kneeling in front of her. All she could feel was numbness.

"Could you help me get Cat out of Mexico?" she asked. Her voice scratched and sounded so odd.

His expression was concerned. He didn't make fun of

her. Maybe he knew she was one step away from the edge, from losing it. "Suppose you tell me what's going on."

Candy lowered her head. She had to trust someone, and she had nowhere to go. She also realized Neil may have already called Rafael at the orphanage, and he could stop her from seeing Cat.

"I left my husband" was all she said before Jim pulled a chair over and sat down in front of her.

"Okay, I guess I saw that coming. So why the need to get her out of Mexico?" He actually reached for her hand and held it. It felt as if someone was listening to her, could hear her voice and was on her side. "Hey, listen, you need to take a breath. First things first, you moved out. Do you have a place to stay?"

She shook her head. She had never gone back into the house to gather anything, instead walking around to where she'd parked the SUV and then driving away. Neil had never come after her. He had let her go, and she hadn't looked back. She didn't have a clue what she'd do next. "I want to help Cat. I want to get her out of Mexico. I want to adopt her. Tell me what I need to do. Please help me …"

"Why the panic, Candy?" He was watching her closely, concerned.

"Neil hired someone to find Cat's family. He found a grandmother, and the mother has two other children." Her throat tightened, and she couldn't finish.

"You're afraid they'll want her back?" he asked. "Candy, I think you need to ask yourself why you're assuming the worst. Do you really believe that, down here, with the poverty, that long-lost family is going to come and claim her, someone with the needs Cat has? No one has been looking for her, have they?"

Candy started shaking her head to get him to stop. She

couldn't take a chance with Cat. The little girl had stolen her heart. "I want Cat. I want to make her mine. I want to get her to Arizona, to your friend the doctor, and help her have everything. I want to get her that implant you were talking about so she can hear. I want to give her every chance and opportunity she can't have here. I believe Neil is doing everything he can to keep her away from me, to prevent me from helping her."

He didn't say anything, but he looked away and shook his head, staring at the door for a moment. She couldn't make sense of what he was thinking, but she couldn't shake a sinking feeling.

"Candy, you really believe your husband would go to such lengths? You know he signed the orphan petition. He's given money to the orphanage for Cat, and someone is working with her to teach her to communicate. From what I understand, he'll provide anything to see to her needs. That doesn't sound like the man you're describing. Why are you thinking the worst?"

Listening to him, of course, it sounded as if she was being paranoid. He was right—Neil had done all that. "You're forgetting he hired someone to find her family," she said.

"Good," Jim said, not swayed in the least. "You want to make sure you've covered all the bases so no one can come along years down the road and say they were looking for her. It needs to be addressed now, and it sounds to me as if your husband is taking care of business. That's what I would do. Did he say he was trying to put Cat back with the family that abandoned her?"

She stared at Jim, wondering why he was on her husband's side. She had to think back. Neil had never come right out and said that, even though that was the impression she had. In fact, he had never answered her, which was what he did when he was holding on to something. "He said he was going to see the grandmother."

"And what else?" Jim asked.

She just shook her head. There wasn't anything else. They'd gone right back to fighting about where he wanted her. "He wants me at home by his side as he waits hand and foot on another woman. He expects me to sit by and be happy Maria is in our home, in a bedroom across the hall. I have to sit by and watch him treat her the way he should be treating me. She's in love with him."

"And you're worried because your husband has acted inappropriately. Has he encouraged her or acted on anything?"

"You're the one who told me of the problems with this surrogacy," she said. Neil had been kind and helpful to Maria, and he was hurting her by not keeping Maria at arm's length. It was one thing to have her carrying his child, but he was waiting on her, watching over her. It was him rather than a hired hand who was always with her. Really, what it came down to was that Neil continued to make decisions without talking to her, and these were the kind of decisions she couldn't live with anymore.

"I'm trying to be objective here. I may not like your husband and how he treats you like a possession instead of a partner, and I wouldn't do what he's done, bringing in a surrogate, but I'm not going to jump on this bandwagon. If you're leaving your husband, make sure you know clearly the reasons, and don't cloud the facts, because I've learned the hard way that, sometimes, things aren't as they seem. You need to ask yourself what the real issue is, Candy. You need to think about everything. Maria and this baby she's carrying, the little girl in an orphanage who will need everything that you have … You need to be really clear before you do something you'll regret."

She stood up. Was he on Neil's side? She couldn't believe it. "Thanks, Jim," she said. "I'm sorry. Maybe I shouldn't have come here."

"Okay, stop," he said. He was standing in front of her, his hands on her shoulders, holding her so close … and then he surprised the hell out of her. He stepped in, sliding his hands over her cheeks, not in a gentle way, and he kissed her deeply. It was so fast she didn't have time to think, but when he pulled back, she just stared at him, breathing. There was nothing there with Jim. Even the taste of him didn't stir anything in her. Maybe he knew, as he stepped back, allowing his hands to fall to his side. "Sorry—or maybe I'm not, Candy. You have to know how I feel about you. You couldn't cheat on your husband even if you wanted to—could you? I guess I already knew that."

She felt her face heat. As charming and nice and handsome as Jim was, she didn't want him touching her like that or kissing her again. She really liked him—she liked talking to him, maybe because he listened to her. She wished for a minute that she could feel something for Jim, as she was positive a life with him would be easier, but there was no burning need to have him touch her, even though she'd wondered what it would be like to kiss a man like Jim, to be with him. Maybe it was that saying: The grass is always greener on the other side. The fact was that Neil was in her blood so deeply she wondered whether she'd ever get him out.

"I'm sorry," she said.

"No, I'm sorry," he replied. She could see the distance between them now. Everything seemed so out in the open. "Your husband is a very lucky man … and a fool." He stepped away from her and reached in his pocket to pull out a set of keys, dangling them in front of her. "Take them," he said. "I have a spare room. You can stay there as long as you need to."

She stared at the keys as the reality of the situation set in. If she took them and stayed with Jim, it really would be over with Neil.

Maybe he sensed her hesitation, as he went to his desk and scribbled something on a piece of paper, setting the keys on top. "Here's my address. You'll be safe there, and I promise I won't do anything inappropriate." He pulled open the door and lingered for a moment. "I have patients to see," he said, and then he left her with one of the biggest decisions she'd ever have to make.

Chapter 25

S itting in the dark in an old easy chair in the corner of the small room, she took in the night setting in outside the small windows. Her mind had gone to some pretty dark places today as she imagined a life without Neil—but she had also gone back over everything that had brought her and Neil together to begin with, including all the misunderstandings, the jealousy, and her ideas about what he really wanted.

If it hadn't been for Neil, she wouldn't be alive today. He'd saved her when the hurricane had ripped through after she'd refused to evacuate. Instead of walking away and leaving her, he'd dug in and kept her safe. That was what she loved about him, his sense of duty, his need to protect those he cared about. He was overbearing and so strong willed at times that she wondered whether she really had what it took to be with him. She wasn't like her sisters-in-law, Diana and Emily, who had figured out a way to be with their strong-willed Friessen men. They made it look so easy, the way they had their men believing they were making all the decisions when, in fact, those strong, stubborn women had figured out how to love their men without allowing them to take away who they were. It was an art she was positive she wasn't strong enough to pull off.

Maybe that was why she hadn't gone home.

She stared at the keys in her hand. Using them and staying with Jim, she knew, meant she would be doing the same thing Neil was now doing to her. It would be pouring salt in their wounds. With Neil moving Maria in, it had seemed as if he was trading Candy for another woman, but she wasn't one of those women who jumped from one man to another. Even though Jim's offer was platonic and decent, she knew Neil well enough to know he'd never believe Jim's intentions had been noble. There were just some lines you didn't cross with your man.

Candy gazed at Cat, who was fast asleep in one of the new beds Candy had purchased. There were six others in the room, but no one shared Cat's single bed, covered with the princess sheets and the doll Candy had bought her. The little girl had lovely brown hair that had shone after Candy brushed it before bed. She was clean and wearing the pink nightgown Candy had also bought her. The little girl had fallen fast asleep, knowing that Candy was there watching over her.

There was a light tap on the door, which was slightly ajar. She slid around, and her heart thudded when she locked eyes with Neil. He wasn't the neat and tidy Neil he usually was. He was dressed in jeans and a t-shirt and a light brown jacket. His hair was unruly, as if he'd been running his hands through it. She slowly rose on shaky legs as he stepped into the room, his gaze sweeping over the children and landing on Cat. Then she noticed Jim behind Neil, who was watching her. In that moment, she felt so guilty, holding those keys. She felt as if she had been caught cheating.

Jim glanced at the children, and she could see the way he stepped back and took her in briefly, without showing any emotion, before he said to Neil, "Out here."

She didn't know what he meant. Neil's face was hard, the way he held his jaw, as if all the hurt between them had come to a head in this moment. He took in Candy and then extended his hand, gesturing for her to come out in the hallway.

They couldn't talk around the kids without disturbing them, of course. Neil pulled the door closed. It was all quiet, and then Jim started down the hall. Neil followed, only glancing down at Candy once.

"Rafael is away tonight. Let's go into his office," Jim said. He was speaking to Neil, and Candy couldn't get past how he had showed up here with her husband as if they'd had a conversation about her. The idea terrified her.

She was trembling as she followed them in and found a spot by the window, leaning against it and crossing her bare arms, which were covered in goose bumps. She hadn't even grabbed a sweater when she left that morning. Maybe Neil had noticed, as he took his jacket off and held it out to her. She saw his hesitation, as if he wasn't going to push but was giving her the chance to take it. She moved away from the wall and allowed him to slip it over her shoulders. It was still warm from him. It smelled of him, and she fisted both ends together and pulled it around her.

She swallowed and looked over at Jim, who glanced at her husband. She could tell that something had transpired between them. Before anyone could say anything, she set Jim's keys on the pastor's desk. Neil's eyes went right to them, and she didn't miss the sharpness and carefully controlled anger lingering just below the surface.

"Jim came to see me, Candy," he said. "He told me how you want to get Cat out of the country, that somehow you think I was trying to reunite Cat with people who abandoned her." He was watching her, and there was a world of hurt between them. "How could you think something like that, after everything we've been through? I'm not a monster."

"But you told me you found her family. You hired someone to find them and you were going to see the grandmother." Her voice was shaking.

"To find out what happened, Candy! This is a little girl who's deaf and can't look after herself, and she was abandoned. I needed to get them to sign away their parental rights so there are no problems waiting to come out of the woodwork. There're a lot of unanswered questions, including why a little girl isn't registered."

"Then what, Neil? You never said anything to me, so what was I supposed to think when you refused to talk to me, to share what you were doing with me?" she said. When she looked over, she saw that Jim was giving all his attention to Neil. It seemed as if some discussion had already taken place, and here she was—still on the outside, looking in. "What?" She gestured between the two of them. "I'm a big girl. Fill me in as to what's going on."

"Your husband met with the grandmother." Jim only glanced her way, then said to Neil, "You better tell her."

"Tell me what?" she asked.

Her husband let out a breath. "Have you really looked at Cat, taken a really good look at her?" he asked.

What was he getting at? She didn't understand, and she frowned.

"Her coloring, Candy," he said. "She's not Mexican. I saw it the first time I laid eyes on her. Look at the other children and then her; light blue eyes ... and even her hair color isn't so dark."

She had a sinking feeling there was something she had missed.

"There are American children down here, Candy, with family back in the US who are looking for them," Jim said, and Candy immediately realized the ramifications.

"You think she's American and has family looking for her?" she said to Jim. Then she glanced over at Neil, who was watching her with what she could only imagine was worry.

"Yeah, I did, Candy," Neil replied. "I spoke with the grandmother. Her daughter, Cat's mother, dropped her off behind that restaurant and waited there until a man found her. She said she knew he was kind and would help Cat, and she followed him to the orphanage. She loves her, but she can't look after her. She's just a vendor—peddling, making clothes that she sells to tourists. She felt she'd be better off here. The father was a US serviceman stationed down here. When he left, she never saw him again."

She wanted to sag against the wall. She had felt so much anger toward Cat's mother, but what would she have done under those circumstances? Maybe everything wasn't as it seemed, but she thought she'd starve herself before she'd ever let her child go. "So what now? They want her back?" she asked. She wanted to weep for Cat, for herself. She felt the tears burn her eyes. Neil blurred in front of her.

"No. The mother has agreed to sign over her parental rights. She's registered, and I have the information." She wondered for a moment, as she watched Neil, was this a trick? "She wants to sign the rights over to us," he clarified as he stepped closer.

The room swayed as she tried to grasp what Neil was saying. She didn't think she had heard her husband correctly.

He stepped closer but didn't touch her. Instead, he jammed his hands in his pockets. "We have permission to take Cat out of the country, to Arizona, where she can have her surgery."

Candy found herself looking at Jim, who leaned against the desk, his arms crossed. He shrugged and gestured to her husband, who'd just blown her world apart again.

Chapter 26

"Are you two okay?" Neil strode down the aisle of the private plane he had chartered. He was dressed so casually, in blue jeans and a black t-shirt. He put a jacket over one of the seats beside the sofa where Candy was sitting, holding Cat in her lap.

The little girl was terrified. She wore a pink sundress that Candy had picked up at the market, with a white sweater overtop, and she clutched the doll Candy had given her.

"Yeah, she's just scared," Candy said to her husband, wishing she could figure out how to get past this distance between them.

He nodded and held on to the chair back as the engine started up. Cat moved and looked around, maybe feeling the vibration. Candy signed that it was okay, everything would be all right.

"What are you saying to her?" Neil asked.

"I just told her it was going to be okay."

Cat signed back and glanced up at Neil.

"What is she saying?" Neil asked.

"She wants to know who you are," Candy replied. She glanced up at Neil as she signed back to Cat, and the little girl smiled up at Neil. She knew Neil was going to ask what she'd said to her. This was a side of Neil she'd never seen before, where she was the one having to explain things to him. "I just told her that you're my husband, and you're making sure she's safe, and you're taking care of us," she said. She couldn't really make out what he was thinking, but she noticed when he looked away that he was fighting to hold it together.

"Mister Friessen, we need you to take your seats," the pilot said, popping into the cabin. "We're ready to go."

"Thank you," Neil replied before turning back to face them. "Candy, seatbelts. Cat has to sit in her own seat." He actually reached for Cat, which left Candy speechless, and Cat let him pick her up. He sat her in the seat facing the sofa, buckled her in, and sat beside her, buckling his own seatbelt. "Candy, put your seatbelt on," he said gently.

She fumbled for her belt for a moment, worrying about whether Cat would panic, sitting next to Neil. She seemed fine, though, and she slipped her tiny hand in Neil's. He took it. She didn't understand any of this or the sudden change in Neil.

Cat fell asleep not long after the flight took off. Neil tilted her seat back and covered her with a blanket, then slid over to the sofa beside Candy.

"I don't understand the change in you, Neil," Candy said. "I don't understand any of this."

From the moment she'd left the orphanage the night before with Neil, Jim had walked the other way without saying another word to Candy. Neither of the two men had seemed willing to tell her what had gone on between them. It wasn't until this morning, when she and Neil had been getting ready to leave, that she realized the bedroom across the hall was empty. Neil hadn't said a word to her about Maria and where she was as they drove to the orphanage and picked up Cat. Still, as she sat here now, beside him, she didn't know what to say, what to ask. She had a million questions, and some she really didn't want to know the answers to.

"What's to understand, Candy? You're my wife, and this is about our life together. I would never do something to intentionally hurt you, and I'm sorry for what's happened. Just let it go, and let us take Cat to Arizona for help. Can't that be enough?" he said, glancing out the window of the plane. She could tell there had to be more, but sometimes Neil just wasn't willing to share. There were times when she shouldn't push, and this felt like one of them.

"What happened between you and Jim?" She had to know.

"Having a man pay me a visit about my wife was something I never pictured happening, Candy. You talked to this man about things you should have talked with me about. You trusted him when you didn't trust me, and yet you were doing the same thing you accused me of."

She could make out nothing but the flash of anger and hurt in his expression. "So what now, Neil?" she asked.

He didn't say anything for a moment, as if considering carefully. "I've rented us a place in Arizona, a furnished apartment close to the hospital. I've already spoken with Doctor Pearson, the neurologist your doctor friend talked about. He'll do the initial workup to confirm that there's enough of the auditory nerve functioning for a successful procedure. As soon as we land, we're meeting with him. He'll walk us through everything we need to know."

She didn't know what to say, but there was something she remembered very well, something Diana and Emily had told her about being married to a Friessen man: She needed to be smart enough and strong enough to know when to stand up to him, when to let him believe something was his idea, and when to let him think he had won. For the first time, she found herself realizing this was one of those times they had been talking about. Whatever had happened in that discussion between Jim Miller and her husband, she realized Neil might never share what had passed between them.

"Thank you," she said, not missing the surprise in Neil's expression.

He didn't reach for her hand or try to touch her on that small sofa as they sat side by side, like two familiar strangers.

Chapter 27

D r. Graham Pearson was a short, dark-haired man in his forties. He wore rimless glasses, a light blue dress shirt, a dark blue tie, and tailored dress pants. He was a sharply dressed man who walked with purpose in his step as he hung up his white doctor's coat on a hook in his office, into which he'd escorted Neil and Candy. It was large, with a sofa and chairs and large plate-glass windows overlooking a mezzanine.

Cat was now in between Neil and Candy, sitting so quiet and still for a little girl. She leaned her head against Candy's breast, and Candy slid her arm around the little girl, holding her against her as if she were her very own.

"Thank you for letting me take a look at Cat," Pearson said. "Just as I suspected, I do agree with the results Doctor Miller sent. There's enough auditory nerve—"

There was a knock on the door.

"Come in," Pearson called out.

The door popped open, and a middle-aged woman wearing a white doctor's coat, with blue scrubs underneath, stepped inside. She had short, dark hair and glasses, and she was plump around the middle. She closed the door behind her.

"Lisa, thanks for coming," Pearson said. "Neil and Candy, this is Doctor Alvariz. She's an otolaryngologist, a head and neck surgeon, who specializes in hearing problems. She's one of the best for cochlear implant surgery, and she's going to walk you through the procedure."

Candy was confused. She glanced toward Neil, and she could tell by the way he was leaning on his elbow, rubbing his chin, that he didn't know what was going on, either.

"I'm confused. I thought you would be doing the surgery," Neil said to Pearson, gesturing between the two doctors.

"No, Doctor Pearson is a neurologist," Alvariz said as she sat in one of the chairs. "He would be doing a surgery if there were no auditory nerve, and we would be looking at a different type of procedure altogether. What I want to do is walk you through the implant procedure. I'll be making an incision behind the ear, where I'll implant a wire."

"So when she wakes up, she'll be able to hear?" Candy asked.

Neil actually reached over and touched her hand. "No, that's not the way it works," he said, and she looked at Neil, surprised that he knew so much.

"The cochlear implant is two parts," Alvariz said. "It will be a few weeks before a receiver is put on the outside of the ear, and it attaches like a magnet." She was leaning forward, and she paused as if wondering whether they understood what she was saying. When no one said anything else, she continued. "The hairs inside the ear are like piano keys. Each one produces a different vibration, and sound notes are transmitted to the brain. When these are damaged or—as in Cat's case—missing, no sound is transmitted. A few weeks after the surgery, an audiologist will come in and attach the receiver. It will not be turned on, as our first step is getting her used to wearing it. It's like a hearing aid, and this device is what picks up the sound. The internal part transmits the sound to the brain, and the device has to be programmed."

The doctor was talking to Neil and Candy, and Candy saw that her husband seemed to understand what she was saying.

"And the therapists will start how soon after?" he asked.

Candy knew her husband was smart, but she wondered, with the way he was asking questions and talking, whether he had researched the details of this procedure.

"There'll be a team, and for months we'll be doing programming, rehabilitation, speech therapy. It's very important that you understand that once this is turned on, you want to expose her to your voice, the sound, by reading and talking. You need to get the information to her brain."

Neil was nodding, and Candy just sat there, taking it all in.

"So what you're saying is that we're here in Phoenix for the duration of this therapy, and we're talking months?" she asked. She hadn't really thought past tomorrow and the surgery, but when Neil glanced over at her, it finally sank in—he had just moved them to Phoenix.

Chapter 28

The apartment turned out to be a three-bedroom, two-thousand-square-foot penthouse suite five blocks from the hospital. It was completely furnished, comfortable and modern, and the master suite had the best feature of all—a king-sized bed. There were also floor-to-ceiling tinted windows, with an en suite bathroom with a huge sunken tub that could easily fit half a dozen people. Candy should have known Neil wouldn't settle for anything ordinary.

Neil was carrying Cat, murmuring to her even though she couldn't hear a thing. It was sweet, really, the way Cat was watching him. Candy tried to sign to her, but the little girl wasn't looking her way.

Neil was apparently showing her around, and he took her down the hall to another bedroom with a double bed and a dresser. It was a neutral-colored room, a nice size, but definitely not meant for a child.

"She needs toys, Neil," Candy said. "I don't think she's ever had them."

Neil put Cat down, and she just stood there, holding

her doll. Candy was feeling nervous, and she wondered if Cat was, as well. Maybe that was why she was staring at her and then Neil.

"I'll order some toys, clothes, whatever she needs and have them sent over," he said. "What do you think she wants?"

"I don't know. Maybe more dolls, some coloring books, crayons," she said, noticing the distance between her and Neil was a couple feet, if not more. She could have moved closer to him and reached out, but she didn't know how he'd react, so she gave her attention to Cat and signed to her, asking her if she was hungry.

"What are you saying?" Neil asked.

When she glanced up, she could tell he was uneasy. Cat signed back to her, and she had to smile. "She's hungry. I'm not sure what food we have, though. She was wondering if we could look in the magic fridge in the kitchen," she replied, and she took in the puzzled expression on Neil's face. "That huge, stainless steel fridge you showed her when we walked through."

"Ah, that one. Tell her I'll make sure the magic fridge is filled with everything a little girl would love." He then winked at Cat, and Candy signed to her.

Cat smiled brightly with a set of nice white baby teeth. It was then that Candy noticed Neil seemed to be softening to the little girl.

He said, "I'll go grab lunch for us, and groceries." He didn't kiss her as he would have before the tension between them had escalated, but he did gaze at her, and she could tell he might have considered kissing or touching her right before there was a knock on the door.

"Are you expecting someone?" Candy asked as Neil started through the living room to the front door.

He didn't answer, but she could hear whomever he was

talking to. He knew them, and it sounded as if he was happy to see them. She signed to Cat to come with her, and the little girl held her hand and followed her out. Candy was stunned when she noticed Neil's brother, Brad, and his wife, Emily. They had luggage, two suitcases, which Brad set down. Both of them were dressed casually in blue jeans and t-shirts.

"Hey, Candy, good to see you," Emily said as she set her purse down on the sofa. Her hair hung down loose and long, just past her shoulders, and she strode over to Candy and hugged her.

"Hi, Candy," Brad called out as he stood with Neil, his gaze lingering on Cat.

"Who's this?" Emily asked, looking down at Cat. Her eyes were bright when she gazed back up at Candy.

"This is Cat," Candy replied, looking over at Neil, who was standing with his arms crossed, not saying anything. For a moment, she wanted to be angry, because only Neil would do something like this, have his brother and sister-in-law come out here without saying a word to her. And for what purpose? Maybe he realized how mad she was, as he gestured to his brother.

"I called Brad and Emily, told them about Cat, and asked them to come out," he said.

Emily was looking to Brad and then back to Candy, her expression uneasy. "I have a great idea, Candy. Why don't you and I go out and take a walk? I've been sitting for hours and really need to stretch my legs," she said. Candy couldn't leave Cat, and she started to shake her head, but Emily cut in again before she could speak. "Maybe we could take Cat to the park? There has to be one around here."

"There's one out back, behind the complex. If you two do that, Brad and I'll hit the store, get some groceries," Neil said, but the look Brad gave his brother was priceless.

"That should be interesting, considering Brad really doesn't know his way around a grocery store," Emily teased.

Brad was shaking his head, grinning. "I know my way around a grocery store. You just do a better job, is all." He actually walked over and kissed Emily before heading back over to Neil and putting his hand on Neil's shoulder. "Let's go, Neil. I hope you have a car, since we took a cab from the airport."

Neil started toward the door, not bothering to kiss Candy goodbye or say anything else. The look they exchanged was awkward.

<h1 style="text-align:center">Chapter 29</h1>

Candy pushed Cat on the swing in the lovely community park right behind the condominium. It wasn't overly crowded, and there were maybe six children scattered over the area.

"We were surprised to get Neil's call," Emily said. She sat in the swing beside Cat, holding the chains and taking in the area.

"I didn't know he called you, but then, Neil doesn't tell me much of anything," Candy said.

Emily was watching her with concern. "I wondered, but walking into that apartment, anyone could see the trouble between you two. Brad mentioned it a time or two over the last month. He's been concerned about you two and what's been going on," she said. Maybe it was the expression on Candy's face that had Emily adding, "They talk often—every week. Keeping in touch is important to Brad. For so long, he was distant with the family because of his first wife, Crystal, who put a rift in the family, between the brothers. It was especially bad with Rodney. They didn't speak for years." She shook her head and glanced away. "I know he goes out of his way now to make sure they stay in touch."

Candy had never really asked about Brad's first wife, although she knew enough from Neil to know that she no longer played a part in the life of their son, Trevor, and she apparently wasn't very nice. "Did Neil ask you and Brad to come?" she said. She needed to know, and she was so tired of Neil just doing things without talking to her.

"Maybe, but not in so many words. When we heard you were using a surrogate to have a baby, both Brad and I worried that you hadn't thought through the potential problems. I know Brad was calling Neil to check in often, and Neil, being Neil, kept telling Brad everything was fine." Emily was watching her, maybe to see her reaction.

"I didn't want a surrogate," she said, still pushing Cat.

"Ah, I see. I can't say I would go for that if I were in your shoes, either. Even Brad was concerned, and he told me he was pretty sure his brother was steamrolling you again."

Maybe Candy's stunned expression showed on her face. She hadn't realized that Brad even noticed or cared.

"We noticed—or Brad did, at least," Emily said. "Then again, he does that to me, too. He just doesn't realize it." She smiled. "When you were in the hospital after the hysterectomy, Brad had a talk with Neil and told him that even if he parted ways with you and took off, as far as he was concerned, you were still family. He told Neil he'd make sure you were looked after, and he had every intention of seeing you brought back to the ranch. My husband takes his role seriously. We wouldn't turn our backs on you."

Candy was speechless. She gripped the chain of the swing when Cat slipped off and then wandered to the sand and started playing with the plastic pails that had been left there, filling them up with the soft white sand using a small plastic shovel. "I didn't know that," she said, her throat feeling a little tight.

"Ah, the Friessen men, they're a challenge, but I wouldn't trade my husband for anything. I've had the other option. My ex-husband was … not Brad," she said, smiling again. She really was beautiful, and Candy wondered how she did it. Even with Trevor, who had autism, and their two other girls, she made everything look so easy.

"I wondered, when you walked through the door, if Neil had called you because of Cat and her disability," Candy said. She crossed her arms and looked down at Cat when Emily didn't answer. "I never knew how you did it with Trevor. It wasn't that he scared me, but I didn't know how to talk to him or what to expect."

"Most people don't, but he's come so far. He'll be in puberty soon. His teen years are so close, so we need to have a different game plan. Is he going to have his own life, be independent?" She smiled, but there was a sadness there that Candy had never seen in Emily before. "Rodney called us, said there was trouble. He was the one who told us that Neil had moved the surrogate into the house and you weren't handling it well—which, I can tell from your face, is an understatement. Yesterday, Brad got a call from Neil to tell him you had left him, and he mentioned then this little deaf girl you were visiting at the orphanage. That was when Brad told me to pack our bags, and I called in a friend to stay with the kids."

"I don't know what's going through Neil's mind," Candy said. "He did move Maria in, and now she's in love with him. This is their baby, and I can't have any part of that, but when he showed up at the orphanage with Jim …" She stopped when she noticed the strange expression on Emily's face. "Jim Miller is the doctor who figured out

Cat was deaf when everyone else said she was intellectually disabled," she explained. She didn't add in the fact that she and Jim were friends and that there had been something between them that was beyond a professional relationship, at least where Jim was concerned.

"I see," Emily replied.

"I love Neil," Candy said. "I would never cheat on him."

Emily just watched her, and then maybe she decided to let it go. "You two have this magnetic, powerful, unique love that at times seems almost destructive. You need to be careful, Candy, that you don't lean elsewhere when you should be leaning on your husband."

Candy had reminded herself of the same thing over and over again. Had she encouraged Jim? They had become confidants, not much different from how Neil was with Maria. "I hear you," she said. "I know you're right."

Emily looked over at Cat. "And now you're here, and Neil has arranged for this surgery for Cat, and he's moved all of you to Phoenix for the duration. What about the surrogate?" Emily asked as Candy sat in the swing next to her.

Candy looked over at her sister-in-law, the one person who had been at her bedside when she woke up from the hysterectomy and had stayed with her at the hospital. She shook her head. "I don't know. Neil arranged this, and when we went home and Maria was gone, I didn't ask. To be honest, I'm afraid of the answer."

Emily nodded. "You know Neil loves you. However this started out, you have to find a way to dial it back, get back to each other. Remind yourself of the love you have for each other."

"Is it enough?" Candy said. "He wants children, Emily, and I don't believe anymore that loving me is enough for him. He wants a child of his own, with his blood, that's a part of him—and I want Cat." She watched the little girl play so quietly, and Emily smiled over at her.

"She's beautiful, Candy. This is the first time I've seen you so comfortable around a child. She's lucky to have you."

"I'm the lucky one," Candy said. She cleared her throat. "I want to adopt her, and I don't know where that'll put me and Neil."

Emily reached over and took her hand. "Then you need to sit down with Neil, no distractions, and you need to talk with him. Make him listen, Candy. I know you can do it. I can't believe Neil wouldn't want to be a part of this, as well. Look at what he's done, what he's arranged, and where you are. I know, better than anyone, that a man doesn't do all this for a child if he doesn't care."

Candy took in the playground. Cat was going to have her surgery, and they were living in Phoenix. Emily was right. The only problem was that she didn't know whether Neil was doing this out of obligation or because he genuinely cared for Cat.

Chapter 30

Candy closed the door to their bedroom. She could hear the shower running, and she hesitated, her hands sweating as if this was the first time she had ever been alone with Neil. The door to the bathroom was ajar, and Candy found herself crossing the room. She paused outside the bathroom and then swallowed before stepping into the steamy room, seeing Neil in the glassed-in shower—naked.

The water turned off, and he opened the door. She blushed as she took in all six feet of leanness and muscle. He kept himself athletically toned, with dark hair on his chest and six-pack abs that her gaze went right to. She loved running her hands over all that hardness and feeling it pressed against her naked breasts. He glanced at her as he reached for a towel and began drying himself off. If he noticed her discomfort, he didn't say anything. He looped the towel around his slim hips and went to the sink, brushing his teeth while Candy stood there, trying to get her tongue to move.

He rinsed his mouth and wiped it with a hand towel,

then turned around, leaning against the sink. He crossed his arms but didn't say anything.

"Why didn't you tell me you were talking to your brother, that he and Emily were coming?" Candy asked. He started out of the bathroom as if he didn't want to answer her, but she grabbed his arm with both hands. "No, you're not going anywhere. You're not dismissing me or ignoring me. You are *not* walking away from me." She actually dug her heels in and pulled him back. Then she shut the door and blocked it with her back against it. If he wanted to leave, he'd have to physically move her.

He actually had the nerve to chuckle under his breath.

She fisted her hand and shoved it against his chest. "Don't laugh at me, either! You're not leaving this bathroom until you talk to me and tell me everything that's going on in your head, what you're thinking, what you want from me. And Cat, what about her? You brought us all the way to Phoenix and arranged for her surgery, and we're living here now, but you never said anything to me. I want to know what you've planned. Tell me, Neil, everything, because I won't allow you to put her back in that orphanage after her surgery. I want to adopt her."

There, she had said it. Neil appeared tired, and she wondered if he'd finally open up and talk to her or if he'd find a way to push her aside.

"You're my wife, Candy, and I made a vow to love you, cherish you, and protect you, but when I saw you in the orphanage that night, you had another man's keys in your hand, a man who's interested in you. Were you considering turning to him?" Neil gritted his teeth, and she could see the carefully controlled rage—as well as something else. She realized she had hurt him.

"I had his keys, but I never used them. I couldn't. I love you, and I'm not a cheater. He left them for me and offered me a spare room, Neil, that's all. I never went there, and I hope you know that, because you found me at the orphanage. Whatever you did with Maria, moving her in … I just couldn't cross that line with Jim. I hope you know that he offered the room as a friend."

Neil shook his head. Didn't he believe her?

"What about Maria, Neil? She wasn't at the house. I'm afraid to ask, because I don't want to know anymore, nothing more about her—"

"She lost the baby," he stated. "It was a miscarriage after all. She's gone." He said it so matter of factly, so coldly, that she wondered whether this was his way of dealing with it. She knew how much he wanted that baby, what it meant to him. This had to be eating his guts out.

"I'm sorry, Neil. I know how much you wanted that baby." She was sorry for his pain, but not that Maria had lost the baby. She couldn't say that, though, not to Neil. He wouldn't understand. She looked away.

"Cat won't be going back to the orphanage," Neil said after a moment. "Your doctor friend made me see how much you care for this little girl. I guess I already knew, deep down, but didn't want to admit it. You've had trouble taking to children, yet this little girl came along, needing so much more than a typical child, and you were all in. I guess I finally realized that if I gave you an ultimatum, Cat or us … you may have chosen Cat."

"Why does it have to be a choice, Neil?" she asked, feeling so sad for what they once had.

"I want a family, Candy, and I just didn't want to listen to your worries. At first, I thought it was because you were scared of children, so I thought I would make it easy and just make the decisions." He was shaking his head. "It doesn't matter anymore. It really is a moot point."

"So what about Cat, Neil? You still haven't answered me."

He gave her an awkward smile that didn't quite reach his eyes. "I guess you better teach me sign language so I can talk to her."

"So does that mean … ?" She was afraid to say it, and maybe he understood, as he stepped closer, putting his hand on her shoulder. Her eyes went right there to where he was touching her, then up to his face and the soft expression there.

"Yes, we're adopting her," he said.

She didn't think when she threw her arms around his neck, pressing herself against him. His hands went around her, holding her to him, and she kissed him softly at first, then deeper.

Chapter 31

SEVEN MONTHS LATER

Cat's surgery had been a simple procedure, but the process after had been grueling for her—or at least that had been how Neil experienced it. She had cried while waking up, and Candy had slipped into bed and held her. It had been difficult to communicate with her when she was still groggy from the anesthetic.

Neil was positive there had been at least a dozen times he wanted to put a stop to the entire procedure. It had broken his heart to watch what Cat had to go through. The way the doctors had explained the procedure, it had sounded simple and straightforward—that was, until you had to put a four-year-old child through it. First was the discomfort of the incision, then watching for infection, then the side effects, which included dizziness from the implanted wire. The first time she had been fitted with the receiver was only after long hours of therapy, but worse than anything was that she'd been terrified when they turned on the sound. For Neil, who had perfect hearing, it was difficult to understand what it must have been like for a child who had been living in silence and suddenly had all this noise to decipher. He just couldn't imagine how horrible, scary, and awful it must have been. He had almost cried.

Candy *had* cried. He'd lost count of the number of times. Her vulnerability had made way for a new closeness between them, and he'd finally seen their walls come down. He loved Candy, even though he had considered letting her go the day she had walked away from him. In those few seconds after she left, he'd really had to think about what was more important, Candy or his baby. For a while, he had hated her for making him have to choose.

But his father had been right. Rodney had pulled him aside and reminded him that he'd made a promise to Candy, and a Friessen man lived and died by his word. Candy didn't deserve to have Maria shoved in her face, and maybe it had taken Jim Miller showing up on his doorstep and sucker punching him in the stomach to make him understand that. The man had knocked the wind out of him, and Neil had been ready to kill the bastard or seriously hurt him when Jim Miller grabbed him by the shirt, shouting, "You don't deserve her!"

He had known then that Jim was in love with his wife, and having another man show up and tell him what an ass he'd been and how badly his wife was hurting, as if he'd chosen to replace her with another woman … well, maybe that had been the wakeup call he'd needed. He felt like crap, and after everything he and Candy had been through, he couldn't let her go. The thought of another man, Jim Miller, having a shot at his Candy and spending any time with her … Neil was having none of that. No matter where he and Candy were right now in their troubles, he couldn't allow any door to remain open for Jim Miller to slip in and find a way to take his wife. That wasn't going to happen, so Neil had done the only thing he could. He had made arrangements to get his wife and the little girl that had been an albatross between them out of the country. He had just never expected to fall in love with Cat.

He prayed that Candy never found out what a selfish bastard he'd been. He had listened to her sweet, soft voice as she read one of the hundreds of books he'd bought for Cat. He could have bought stock in a children's bookstore for the amount he had spent on her, Candy had teased him, but Neil couldn't help himself from wanting to give Cat everything in the world.

Every day, Neil and Candy read to Cat, exposing their voices to her, getting the sound and as much information to her brain as they could. He signed to Cat when he talked to her, and she watched his lips when he spoke, but the first time she'd said "Daddy" in her odd voice, he had pulled her in his arms and cried. Candy had been there, and there had been something about his vulnerability in that moment that had opened her heart to him.

He lingered outside Cat's bedroom now. He had transformed it into a room a princess would love. The furniture was from the Cinderella line at the local furniture store, all white with toys and stuffed animals everywhere, and he watched as his daughter, the little girl who would be theirs officially at the end of the year, absorbed every word and every sound, everything Candy said to her. He could sit for hours, he thought, and watch Candy be a mother to Cat. Her confidence, the love that poured out of her … he couldn't picture any other woman giving the kind of love to their child that Candy could.

The phone rang, and Candy looked up.

"I've got it," Neil said with a smile, letting her know with just a look what she meant to him—and he intended to show her later, when Cat was asleep. He was whistling as he started down the hall and grabbed the portable phone from the sofa table. "Hello?"

"Neil?" The connection wasn't that great.

"Yes, this is Neil Friessen," he said, distracted. He wanted to laugh and race back down the hall when he heard Cat repeat something Candy had said. He didn't want to miss any of it, and he had taken two steps closer to her room when the man on the other end said, "This is Les Feldman." Neil hesitated and really focused in on the call.

"Your baby has been born," Les said.

Neil shut his eyes, feeling none of the joy that he thought he would. He turned around and went into their master bedroom, closing the door.

"Neil, are you still there?" Les asked, the connection on the line a little clearer.

"Yes, I am. Sorry about that, Les. I didn't recognize your voice. Bad connection, I guess. So the mother is fine, and the baby?"

"Neil, Maria is fine. You have a son. She's been asking for you. Will you come back to Cancun?"

He was shaking his head even before he said anything else. "No, I won't be coming. Did she sign away her parental rights?"

He sighed on the other end. "Yes, she agreed to your terms. She'll sign if you come and see her, and she wants to be able to see the baby now and then, to know how the child is doing—pictures, you know," Les stated.

Neil did know. He pulled the phone away. Candy had been so right about the problems with Maria, but at the time, he just hadn't been able to see it. She had tried to tell him it wouldn't be as easy as he'd made it sound. Maria had held all the cards, his baby … and he, the fool, had let her. He shut his eyes to close off any feeling he'd once had toward Maria. He couldn't allow this to happen again.

He'd just gotten his wife back. They had a little girl he loved more than life itself, and he couldn't live with seeing the agony in his wife's eyes again.

"No, we cut the ties, Les. Maria agreed to all of this in the beginning. You know it, and I know it. She's been changing the agreement from the start. I've sent her money. I've bought a house for her and her mother," he hissed. "You tell her that if she signs this, she'll get one more check from me."

"You've paid her a lot of money. How much more are you willing to give her?" Les said.

"Five million," Neil stated, listening to a clatter on the other end.

"That won't leave you with much, Neil," Les said cautiously. "You won't be able to finish your resort, and that little girl … how much have you already spent on her?"

"Cat is my daughter, Les. I would spend everything on her. Les, the resort is almost done, and I'll sell it if I have to. This is the price of love, isn't it?" he said. He didn't wait for Les to respond. "Tell her, Les, that this is my last offer. Sign it, and then you start the adoption."

Les was speaking to someone in the background, and Neil heard a door close.

"Les?" he snapped.

"Sorry, Maria is with her mother," the lawyer replied. "Neil, five million is a lot of money."

Neil sighed. Would he ever be rid of Maria?

"Don't worry," Les finally said. "She's just agreed to the money and your terms."

"I'll be in touch, then—and my son?"

"I'll get the paperwork and the adoption process started. How do you want to handle getting the child?"

"I'll fly back when the baby's ready. Notify the hospital

I'll pick him up. Just make sure Maria has signed away her parental rights."

"Will your wife be coming, too?"

"No. And one more thing—all of this stays between you and me."

His lawyer sighed on the other end. "Neil, does Candy know what you've done about Maria?"

He was shaking his head and moved the receiver from his mouth. "Just get it done, Les! Call me when the baby's ready."

Neil held the disconnected phone and stepped out of the master bedroom.

"Hey, I was looking for you!" Candy said, leaning over Cat, who was now at the coffee table, coloring in one of her books. "Who was on the phone?"

"Well, good news," Neil began. "That was—there's a baby available for adoption, a baby boy … and he's ours." He had her attention, and she stood up. Before she could say anything, he said, "He was just born, and he needs a family."

"A baby has come up for adoption?" she said. Slowly, she tilted her head and smiled. "So when do we get him?"

"Any day. Are you okay with that? Can you be ready?"

She walked around the table and went right into his arms. "Yes, we'll be ready," she said.

Neil held her, his wife, the love of his life, and he kissed her cheeks, her forehead, her nose. "I love you. How do you think Cat is going to like being a big sister?"

Candy glanced at their little girl, the cochlear implant behind her ear, and said, "She's going to be an amazing big sister, but then, she's got a daddy who will do anything for her."

As Neil held her tightly, she closed her eyes. She had been right. He would do anything for his family.

Turn the page for a sneak peek of
A DIFFERENT KIND OF LOVE the next book in *THE
FRIESSENS: A NEW BEGINNING*
Available in print, eBook and audio

A Different Kind of Love

**The bonds of motherhood always run strong…
sometimes too strong in this riveting
contemporary romance.**

**An abandoned child finds a new life with his
father. But his mother who left him suddenly
wants him back. Can the Friessens sort out the
mess and restore their happiness?**

From NY Times & USA Today bestselling author
Lorhainne Eckhart comes a heartwarming and emotional
story about a family faced with secrets and an unexpected
visitor who could destroy their happily ever after. "A
wonderful love story not only about an unconditional love
between a man and woman, but an unconditional heart-
filled love for a special child." (S. George)

"Best Family Series Ever! I love the dynamic of this
powerful close family. Three brothers, a cousin and

all the spouses and children make for an interesting spellbinding story you won't want to put down."

"Author Lorhainne Eckhart is adept at showing deeply felt emotions through actions, instead of just telling us." —

NATASHA JACKSON, READERS FAVORITE

A DIFFERENT KIND OF LOVE brings back the couple you fell in love with in The Forgotten Child. Now, years later, Brad and Emily are faced an entirely new set of challenges with their preteen autistic boy when his mother, Crystal, returns. She wants a relationship with the boy she abandoned—something Brad and Emily never expected. She says she's changed, but can the Friessens believe her?

Chapter 1

She swore it had happened overnight, a shift from hot days and comfortable mornings to a noticeable chill in the air. It was earlier than usual, this very distinct change in seasons from summer to fall. Emily preferred easing in gently, being given time to adjust, over always feeling as if she was on a roller coaster ride and couldn't get off. But this was her life, and if given a choice between this one or one completely different and easy— well, she wouldn't change it for anything. She was human, though, and there were days she wished for nothing but peace.

She could hear the creak of floorboards upstairs where she'd left her husband, Brad, sleeping. He would be wondering where she was when he reached for her. That was just the way it was between them in the mornings, even though they slept curled against one another, his legs entwined and twisted with hers. There wasn't a part of him she didn't love to touch and feel against her. He was the first man to truly have her heart.

He loved her, she loved him, and their children meant

everything to them. This was her family, and it was good—better than good. It was amazing. She loved them all: their little girl Becky, the one child Brad and she shared together, and Katy and Trevor, who were their children from their first marriages. Now she was Trevor's mother, and Brad was Katy's father.

He was on the stairs now. "Em?"

She still loved the sound of his voice; after all these years, he still had the ability to turn her insides to putty. It was so deep and masculine and sexy that she had to fight the urge to run to him, which was something people might call her crazy for if she ever admitted it.

He pushed open the screen door, and she took in his frown from where she leaned against the pillar, bathed in streaks of pink and yellow from the rising sun. "Why didn't you answer me?" He slid his arms around her from behind, pulling her to him, running his flattened palm over the cotton of her nightgown, rubbing against her stomach.

She leaned back into him. He was so warm, and she couldn't imagine ever tiring of the way he held her and how she fit so easily against him. The strength in his arms … she loved running her hands over them, feeling the contrast of the muscle and soft skin and dark hair. He made her feel so secure, as if nothing bad could ever touch her. She sighed in his embrace. He had pulled on a light blue shirt, and its freshly laundered scent mixed with his warmth soothed and stirred her at the same time.

He swayed with her, holding her. She could feel the cut of his biceps, triceps, and pecs, his solid abs pressed against her back. She pictured the feel of them as if they were burned into her memory. She loved to run her hands over all that hardness. She barely passed his shoulders, and he leaned his chin against the top of her head. They rocked together.

"What's wrong?" He pressed a kiss to her forehead, and she breathed him in again. His scent always grounded her.

"I don't know," she replied—and she really didn't. She had woken early and hadn't been able to go back to sleep. An odd stirring feeling had unsettled her. She could feel Brad try to pull back, so she held more tightly to his arm. "No, just hold me like this."

"Are you not feeling well?" He wasn't going to let it go, but then, Brad wasn't a man to just ignore things, not with his family and never with her.

Any fights they had stemmed from him not letting things go. He pushed at times, never letting her hold on to things and sulk. Not that she did. He prodded, always knowing when something was bothering her. They were so in tune with each other. He had such a need to protect her and their children, to the point that she sometimes worried about what would happen if she ever had to stand on her own two feet.

"I couldn't sleep," she said. "Maybe I'm just over-thinking things, with school coming up. I'm just …" She couldn't figure out how to put into words this unsettling feeling that kept coming at her over and over. Something wasn't right, but she couldn't put her finger on it or explain it to Brad in a sane way.

"You're doing too much again," he said. "I told you to stop planning everything. The kids are back in school. Just let them go." He always made it sound so easy—typical man, thinking everything that worked out wasn't the result of some hardworking woman behind the scenes, planning, organizing, and doing.

"Our little girl is going into first grade, and she's going to be gone all day." Emily's throat thickened.

He didn't laugh at her, and she was so grateful for that.

Maybe he understood. "We could have another baby if you want, and then you'd have your hands full again."

It wasn't as if she hadn't thought about it. "I don't know, Brad. Do you want another?" They hadn't tried to have another baby after Becky was born, and she had been completely unplanned. It wasn't that they were being careful or anything now—just that it hadn't happened since.

"You know I would love a houseful, but you're their mother, and most of the work falls to you, honey."

She knew he loved children and he was their protector, but he had a ranch to run, too. She didn't know if she wanted to start over again with diapers and toddlers and not a moment to herself. Although she wouldn't trade one moment of the time she had with her children, she also realized she had more freedom now, and she didn't want to give it up. "Katy is in gymnastics twice a week now, and Trevor … we need to meet with the school again. His consultant is coming out next week to meet with his teacher to get everything started for the new year. There's just so much to do, Brad."

"Hey, Trevor is fine. You see how far he's come, Em. School's going good. Don't start finding things to worry about. You have everyone so organized that nothing can go wrong," he said. At times, she thought, he didn't worry enough.

"Brad, every year we've had something with the school … some problem, some new teacher who wants to change how we do things, and I have to start at the beginning. Remember two years ago when we had that new teacher who refused to work with our consultant or to make any changes in her teaching methodology to accommodate Trevor? She refused every one of the suggestions we made. I thought you were going to lose it," she said.

She could feel him tense behind her. Sitting with Brad in that meeting room at the school, that had been the first time Emily ever thought he could come unglued. She'd made an excuse to get him out of there: "Don't you have a golf game you're going to be late for?" He didn't golf, of course, but he was sharp enough to pick up on her meaning, and he had nodded and left. When she got home, she had barely walked through the door before he gave her an earful, cursing that teacher with every imaginable fate as he paced the kitchen like a wild beast. He'd calmed down eventually, four hours later. Then the principal had phoned, apologizing profusely and assuring them he'd find a way to make it work. He had, but only when he was teaching. It had been a lost year, and without the education assistant who worked with him in the classroom, Trevor would have learned nothing.

"You don't know that, Em. Besides, we already met the teacher, and you said you liked her."

She could feel her heart tightening. She knew it was just her anxiety working overtime, but maybe he could feel it too, as he kissed her ear and slid his hand up and over her heart, her breast, pressing her closer to him. "I know," she replied. "And I'm sure I'm just expecting the worst, all these back-to-school anxieties. It's just that Trevor has come so far. He's independent in so many things; I don't want someone coming in and screwing it up."

He actually chuckled in her ear, and this time she slid around, taking in the humor in his amazing whiskey-colored eyes. They reached inside her, and they had a connection so deep that she couldn't hide anything from him, even if she wanted to. He had this way of making her feel … better.

"Why are you laughing at me?" she said.

"Em, our kids are so lucky to have you for a mother,

and God help any person who tries to come in and mess with them." He slid his hand over her cheek, pressing in, and his fingers brushed her ear. She couldn't help leaning in closer. He kissed her, holding her other cheek, pulling her to him as he deepened the kiss, which brought that stirring deep inside her that happened every time he touched her. She needed to connect with him, skin to skin, and only he could satisfy her.

"Why don't we go upstairs for that good-morning wakeup you denied me?"

He kissed her again and started leading her into the house, but she pulled back and whispered, "Don't you have cows to feed?"

"They'll wait," he said, and he had her halfway to the stairs when they heard the first sounds of little feet jumping out of bed.

"Yeah, but the kids won't," she said with a groan, leaning into him.

He patted her bottom and then tilted her chin so she was forced to look at him. "I may have to tie you to the bed just to make sure you're there in the morning."

She rolled her eyes. "As if you'd ever do that."

"Hey, if I wake up and my wife isn't in bed with me again—I may consider it!" he said, and he kissed her just as she heard the pitter-patter of their three kids hitting the stairs.

The law is the law until someone comes after your family.

From *New York Times* & *USA Today* bestselling author Lorhainne Eckhart comes a new Billy Jo McCabe mystery set on a small island town in the Pacific Northwest. On the eve of Police Chief Mark Friessen's wedding, a fierce snowstorm blankets the island, knocking out power, and the

body of a woman is discovered in the church. The only clue is the note in her hand, a list of names— all members of Mark's family.

Mark Friessen has been counting down the days to his wedding to Billy Jo McCabe. Yet only days from Christmas, after their families arrive, a freak blizzard comes out of nowhere and knocks out power on the entire island.

With the island in an emergency and the ferry shut down, no help is arriving anytime soon from the mainland. Mark receives a call to stop into the church where he and Billy Jo are planning on being married the next day, but there he stumbles upon the body of a woman. The only evidence is a note she's clutching. At the top, in all bold, is the word *KILL*, and listed below are the names of everyone he loves, including Billy Jo, his parents, his brothers, their wives, and his two nieces.

With access to the outside world cut off, Mark finds himself up against an invisible enemy who he believes is coming after his unsuspecting family. But Mark has no idea who it is. Where is the killer hiding on the island, why isn't Mark's name on the list, and who is the dead woman? Mark is determined to find the killer and protect his family, whatever it takes…even if it's his *Last Stand*.

Chapter 1

THE LAST STAND

Mark stared at the weekly report of problems, a revolving door of the same people, those he could do something about and those who just got better at hiding their crimes. He heard the knock on his door just as he took a swallow of coffee, and he turned where he was standing beside his desk.

"Hey, Chief," said Carmen. "Just got a call from Lisa Jenkins about a man who's openly threatening her. His hostility is over the top, so much so that she fears for her safety. She said she showed up for a wellness check on his kids and believes he's hurting them and interfering with her taking them."

He just stared at Carmen as she shrugged on her heavy coat, wondering whether he was supposed to know who Lisa Jenkins was. Maybe his expression gave him away. He set down the printed three-page report, which had been waiting on his desk when he walked in an hour earlier.

"Taking kids, wellness checks? You lost me. Who is this?" He let out a heavy sigh, feeling the weight of every-thing. His parents were on their way, his brothers, their families, and Billy-Jo's family. He still needed to pay the restaurant, pick up his new suit, and make sure he stopped in at the church at some point that day to make sure everything was a go for the wedding. He gave his head a shake, willing himself to get back in the game.

"Lisa…" Carmen said. "You know, the junior social worker brought in to help with the rise in the case load? For your fiancée."

Right. He thought Billy Jo had mentioned that at the church before their meeting with the minister who would listen as they said "I do" and officially pronounce them mister and missus. Maybe that was why he was feeling a gigantic pressure right in the middle of his chest. Mark reached for his cell phone on his desk but saw no message from Billy Jo.

"Billy Jo didn't call," he said. "Is she there too?" He had his phone to his ear already, and it was ringing, but it went right to voicemail.

"Hello, this is Billy Jo McCabe, with DCFS. I can't take your call right now. Leave me a message and I'll call you back when I can. If this is an emergency…"

He hung up. Right, she wasn't going in to work that day because Chase and Rose were flying in, and she was doing all the last-minute stuff involving her dress and something else he couldn't remember.

He realized Carmen was still standing there. "No answer." He held his phone up. "I'll come with you. Have you met this Lisa?" He reached for his keys in his drawer and shoved his phone in his pocket, looking to Carmen as he strode over to the coat tree and reached for his black down winter coat. His gun was holstered on his favorite blue jeans, and his sheriff's badge was pinned to his shirt.

"Only once," she said. "She's young. Don't think she's been doing this long. You want to follow me?"

Mark shrugged on his coat. "Yeah. So tell me again who she is and what's going on. Would have thought this would go through Billy Jo. You said this social worker is taking the kids? She's supposed to call us first, or have I missed something?"

Carmen had already pulled open the door to the station and was walking out. A blast of cold swept over him as he glanced back to his dog's empty bed. Billy Jo had Lucky at home. Maybe that was also why he felt so off that day. His routine was being completely screwed up.

"Lacy," he called out.

"I already know," the dispatcher replied. "I took the call and patched it through to Carmen." She was behind her desk, Gail's old desk, and she gestured to him as she stood up. So damn efficient, but he wondered when he'd stop comparing her to Gail. "You'll be at the Clarks'. I got it." She just lifted her hand, and Mark took in Elisha's empty desk, as well, knowing she was already doing rounds on the island.

"Well, good," he said. "If Billy Jo calls, tell her to call me."

He didn't miss what he thought was the hint of a smile tugging at the older woman's lips. Her hair was a mix of dark and white, and he was pretty sure she was as tall as Gail.

He stepped out of the office and kept walking down the steps, feeling the icy chill. The salt on the steps crunched under his cowboy boots. Heavy clouds loomed overhead, but he knew it was too cold for rain.

Carmen was already in the sheriff's cruiser as Mark pulled open the door of his Jeep and started the engine. Carmen backed out, swinging around and flicking on her siren. So they were there, kids in trouble, a desperate situation. Damn, he hated that. He wished Billy Jo had filled him in more on this Lisa.

He followed Carmen as she pulled down a road he was familiar with and took in the houses so close together. Cars pulled over to the side as they flew past another road, more trees and privacy. Carmen pulled up in front of a small older two-story. He could see a man in the doorway, dark skinned, tall, lanky, and a woman on the porch.

Carmen was parked behind a burgundy Hyundai, and Mark stopped in front, turning off his engine, feeling his sidearm. He stepped out of the Jeep, his coat now zipped, and reached for his brown knit hat in his pocket. As he pulled it on, feeling the bite of cold, he strode across the grass, Carmen already two steps ahead of him.

"Thank goodness you're here," the young woman said. "This man is preventing me from doing my job. He's openly harassed me and been verbally abusive…"

"I did no such thing, you lying bitch. You showed up here, coming in my house, disrespecting me," the man cut in. He wore a long-sleeved faded brown shirt and what looked like sweatpants. He had no coat. Mark figured the woman was Lisa, who had called.

"Okay, so what exactly is going on here?" Mark said, resting his foot on the bottom step.

Lisa was young, early twenties, he thought, wearing dark-rimmed glasses and holding a clipboard close to her chest. He glanced once to Carmen, who appeared right beside him. Mark was very aware of the man's anger toward Lisa. He stepped up onto the porch, looking down on her, putting himself between them.

"And you are?" he said to the man.

"That's Nathan Clark," Lisa cut in behind him, and he didn't miss the snark in her tone. He glanced back once to her, knowing Nathan was fisting his hands. Just her opening her mouth had provoked him.

He turned back to Nathan, who looked past him with dark eyes locked on to the short social worker. He knew when a man had been pushed too far. "Nathan, I'm Chief Friessen. We got a call about some trouble…"

The man was already shaking his head and had pulled his arms across his chest. He had to be cold. Mark took in the closed screen door and could hear voices inside, a woman and kids, he thought.

"Look, I don't know what she's yapping on about, but she showed up here, walking through my house, and yelled at me to get away from her when I did nothing. She was the one disrespecting me and my wife. She's going on about us hurting our kids, which is an outright lie…"

"I'm just doing my job," Lisa said. "You have no right to interfere, and that was exactly what you were doing in there, following me right on my heels and yelling at me, scaring me. This is a state matter, and you are interfering—"

"These are my kids," Nathan said. "You coming in here, turning your nose up at me and—"

"Hey, hey, enough," Mark said. "Just cool down, both of you. Nathan, give us a minute." He turned to the new social worker and wondered why Billy Jo hadn't called him. "Come with me. I want to talk to you."

He went down the steps, seeing her legs were bare under her coat. She wore a short dress underneath, he thought, and light brown ankle boots. He gestured to her and then took in Carmen, who said nothing as she stood there. He had only to nod before he heard her say something to the father, who was standing guard at that door.

He turned around, taking in how short Lisa was, about Billy Jo's height. She really looked like a kid. "What's going on here? Billy Jo sent you?" They were far enough away that he couldn't hear what the father was saying to Carmen, but he could see how upset he was.

"I'm the social worker on call today, and this is a wellness check. A complaint came in, and it was given to me. This has nothing to do with Billy Jo, who's away now. Everything will come through me until she's back from her time off."

The way she was looking at him, he realized she didn't have a clue who she was, but then, he knew Billy Jo didn't go around sharing her personal business. Evidently, Lisa wasn't in the know.

"Billy Jo is getting married to me. I'm her fiancé. You should know, filling in for her, that we have a protocol on the island. In any cases where you're removing a child, you are required to contact my office, and a deputy is to accompany you." He kept his voice low.

When she looked up at him, he could see she wasn't on the same page, maybe because she was shaking her head. "With all due respect, Chief, this was not a visit where I planned to take the kids. But, just showing up here and seeing what I saw, I'm alarmed. The condition of the premises, the dirt, the locked doors…and there was feces on the floor. The father is volatile, and the kids appear unbathed. One little girl, who I understand has special needs, appears neglected." She was so damn matter of fact, and he sensed she would argue about everything.

"Volatile? I think you need to be a little more specific about what your concerns are. You suspect abuse, hurting his kids?" He gestured, wondering why she had a clipboard.

"You saw him up there, the way he looked at me, yelling at me. He stalked behind me in the house when I expected answers from him. He was disrespectful…"

Mark angled his head. He wanted to call Billy Jo again, but if he did, he knew her well enough to know she'd likely be in her car and on her way over there. Maybe there was something more about this situation that he didn't know.

"You showed up here about his kids. I'm seeing a father who's trying to protect them. You want to take his kids away? I would be surprised if a father let you do that without fighting back. You want to walk me inside and show me what the issues are?"

The way she pulled the clipboard up close to her chest, he wondered if she'd say no. "Fine, but I'll need your assistance getting the kids out of the house. This is a state decision, and I'm acting on behalf of the state. I'll need to take the kids, all of them, to the hospital for a doctor to look them over."

Then she turned and started walking back to the house, and Mark followed, seeing that Carmen and Nathan were staring at him long and hard.

"I'm going in the house with Lisa," he said. "Nathan, Carmen will stay outside with you. We won't be a minute."

Lisa had pulled open the screen and walked right in, and Mark reached for the door.

Nathan lifted his hands in the air and linked them behind his head in frustration. "Fine. My wife is there."

"How many kids?" he asked. He could hear Lisa inside, speaking with the kind of voice that expected answers, but about what, he didn't know.

"Two girls, two and five," Nathan said.

He only nodded and walked inside, taking in the small entry, the wood floors, an older sectional with piles of clothes on it, a laundry basket, toys and papers scattered on the floor. A woman with dark hair, a few inches taller than Lisa, was holding a towel. Her hair was half out of a ponytail.

"Down here, Chief," Lisa said to him as she gestured to a narrow hall with doors closed. He only nodded at the woman standing there, wide-eyed, a little girl jumping around her with a thumb in her mouth. Then he realized another girl was there, naked, her hair a mess, shoving ripped paper into her mouth.

"No, no, no, Mellie," the woman said and ran over to the little girl to pull the paper from her mouth. The girl squealed and swatted at her.

Mark saw the mother struggling, and he took in something smeared on the wall in the hall. He could smell it from there and knew it was feces. The social worker was looking at him expectantly as she stood by a door locked with a deadbolt, which needed a key, and another door with a sliding bolt.

"Every door here, all four, has a lock on it," Lisa said. "Do they lock the kids in? I'm sure you can smell that a child defecated, and it's on the walls. One has no clothes on, and there's something wrong with the other, too. The place is a mess. The kitchen is not the neatest I've seen, and there's food in the corner on the floor."

He slid the bolt on one of the doors and opened it to see a bathroom—not a mess but reasonable, with a towel on a hook, toothbrushes by the sink, and a bathtub with no shower curtain.

"Look, I don't know what to say," Mark said. "I see the mess. Is there something wrong with the one screaming out there?" He glanced down the hall. Everything in the house felt tense, but then, he supposed having DCFS show up like this only ramped up family problems.

"Special needs, I think. Not really sure, but something is wrong..." She was flipping through her chart, lifting papers and reading, and then she shook her head and let out an exasperated breath. "But, regardless, the care is seriously lacking. I'll need some help getting the kids loaded up. I think I've seen enough here." She clutched her clipboard to her chest. The way she said it had been dismissive, and damn, did he hate this. She brushed past him, leaving him standing there.

"Okay, I'm taking the kids," she said. "Are there car seats? I need clothes on these girls, too…"

She was cold, unfeeling. Nothing about this felt right. The mother wore a look he knew too well, shellshock. He put his hand on the screen door and pushed it open, and Nathan and Carmen both stopped talking and looked at him.

"Your kids in there," he said. "Something wrong with the little girl with no clothes on?"

The man was much calmer now. He wondered what Carmen had said to him. "My older one, she's five. One doctor said she's got autism, another said rett syndrome. Can't keep no clothes on her. She takes them off as soon as they're on."

Mark realized Carmen hadn't looked away from Nathan, yet she said nothing. "You have locks on the doors in there. You lock the kids in?"

Nathan shook his head and gestured. "No, sir, no way. Those locks are to keep Mellie out. She wears a diaper, but we can't keep it on her. We lock the doors because she goes in and wipes her shit on the walls everywhere, so we have to keep her in one small part of the house. Look, we're doing the best we can, but I'm not always here. I have to work off island a lot, and it's just my wife here. My daughter, she screams if you try to brush her hair. Can't get socks on her at all. I tried to explain all that to the social worker in there, but she wouldn't hear none of it…"

"Hey, Nathan, I get it," Carmen cut in. "You just need some help, is all. Sometimes these state workers only check boxes and can't see or hear anything. I know you're just trying to protect your family, and I can hear how upset you are. She probably didn't understand all that. She's not from around here and doesn't know you."

Damn, how did Carmen do that? The door squeaked open behind them.

"Chief Friessen, I'm ready to go," Lisa said. "Can you get some car seats so I can take the kids?" There was something so inexperienced about the social worker. She had so much to learn about people.

"I have car seats, but I want the name of your supervisor," Nathan said.

Lisa was still standing in the doorway. "My direct supervisor is away right now. You want the name of my acting supervisor this week?" Now she sounded way too helpful.

"I do, name and phone number. I'm calling and making a formal complaint about you."

He wondered whether Lisa would say no, but she only shrugged and said, "Sure. Grant—"

"Billy Jo is in charge here. Pretty sure you report to her," Mark couldn't help himself from saying.

Lisa seemed to stiffen and then shook her head. "Ms. McCabe is away, and that's not how the chain of command works. Grant is who I report to right now." Damn, she was so matter of fact. "You have a pen?"

Carmen, bless her, pulled one from her pocket along with paper and handed it to Nathan, who was going to have his kids pulled out of there. Mark listened to her rattle off Grant's name and number.

"I'll help you with the car seats," Mark said to Nathan. He listened to screaming in the house as he followed him down the stairs and over to an older off-white minivan, and all he could think was that nothing about this seemed right.

"Lorhainne Eckhart is one of my go to authors when I
want a guaranteed good book. So many twists and turns,
but also so much love and such a strong sense of family."

(LORA W., REVIEWER)

New York Times & USA Today bestseller Lorhainne
Eckhart is best known for writing Raw Relatable Real
Romance where "Morals and family are running themes."
As one fan calls her, she is the "Queen of the family saga."
(aherman) writing "the ups and downs of what goes on
within a family but also with some suspense, angst and of
course a bit of romance thrown in for good measure."

Follow Lorhainne on Bookbub to receive alerts on New Releases and Sales and join her mailing list at Lorhainne-Eckhart.com for her Monday Blog, all book news, give-aways and FREE reads. With over 120 books, audiobooks, and multiple series published and available at all, retailers now translated into six languages. She is a multiple recipient of the Readers' Favorite Award for Suspense and Romance, and lives in the Pacific Northwest on an island, is the mother of three, her oldest has autism and she is an advocate for never giving up on your dreams.

"Lorhainne Eckhart has this uncanny way of just hitting the spot every time with her books."

(CAROLINE L., REVIEWER)

The O'Connells: *The O'Connells of Livingston, Montana are not your typical family. A riveting collection of stories surrounding the ups and downs of what goes on within a family but also with some suspense, angst and of course a bit of romance thrown in for good measure. "I thought I loved the Friessens, but I absolutely adore the O'Connell's. Each and every book has different genres of stories, but the one thing in common is how she is able to wrap it around the family, which is the heart of each story." (C. Logue)*

The Friessens: *An emotional big family romance series, the Friessen family siblings find their relationships tested, lay their hearts on the line, and discover lasting love! "Lorhainne Eckhart is one of my go to authors when I want* *a guaranteed good book. So many twists and turns, but also so much love and such a strong sense of family." (Lora W., Reviewer)*

The Parker Sisters: *The Parker Sisters are a close-knit family, and like any other family they have their ups and downs. Eckhart has crafted another intense family drama… "The character development is outstanding, and the emotional investment is high…" (Aherman, Reviewer)*

The McCabe Brothers: *Join the five McCabe siblings on their journeys to the dark and dangerous side of love! An intense, exhilarating collection of romantic thrillers you won't want to miss. — "Eckhart has a new series that is definitely worth the read. The queen of the family saga started this series with a spin-off of her wildly successful Friessen series." From a Readers' Favorite award—winning author and "queen of the family saga" (Aherman)*

Billy Jo McCabe Mystery: *The social worker and the cop, an unlikely couple drawn together on a small, secluded Pacific Northwest island where nothing is as it seems. Protecting the innocent comes at a cost, and what seems to be a sleepy, quiet town is anything but.*

Lorhainne loves to hear from her readers! You can connect with me at:
www.LorhainneEckhart.com
lorhainneeckhart.le@gmail.com

In the Charm
Unexpected Consequences
It Was Always You
The First Time I Saw You
Welcome to My Arms
Welcome to Boston
I'll Always Love You
Ground Rules
A Reason to Breathe
You Are My Everything
Anything For You
The Homecoming
Stay Away From My Daughter
The Bad Boy
A Place of Our Own
The Visitor
All About Devon
Long Past Dawn
How to Heal a Heart
Keep Me In Your Heart

The O'Connells
The Neighbor
The Third Call
The Secret Husband
The Quiet Day
The Commitment
The Missing Father
The Hometown Hero
Justice
The Family Secret
The Fallen O'Connell
The Return of the O'Connells
And The She Was Gone

The Stalker
The O'Connell Family Christmas
The Girl Next Door
Broken Promises
The Gatekeeper
The Hunted

The McCabe Brothers
Don't Stop Me
Don't Catch Me
Don't Run From Me
Don't Hide From Me
Don't Leave Me
Out of Time

A Billy Jo McCabe Mystery
Nothing As it Seems
Hiding in Plain Sight
The Cold Case
The Trap
Above the Law
The Stranger at the Door
The Children
The Last Stand
The Charity
The Sacrifice

The Street Fighter
Finding Home

The Wilde Brothers
The One
The Honeymoon, A Wilde Brothers Short
Friendly Fire

Not Quite Married, A Wilde Brothers Short
A Matter of Trust
The Reckoning, A Wilde Brothers Christmas
Traded
Unforgiven
The Holiday Bride

Married in Montana
His Promise
Love's Promise
A Promise of Forever

The Parker Sisters
Thrill of the Chase
The Dating Game
Play Hard to Get
What We Can't Have
Go Your Own Way
A June Wedding

Kate & Walker
One Night
Edge of Night
Last Night

Walk the Right Road Series
The Choice
Lost and Found
Merkaba
Bounty
Blown Away: The Final Chapter
He Came Back

The Saved Series

Saved
Vanished
Captured

Single Titles
Loving Christine